THE KLONDIKE RING

ADVENTURE • NET
#4
THE KLONDIKE RING

Andrea and David Spalding

Whitecap Books

Edited by Carolyn Bateman
Proofread by Elizabeth McLean
Cover design by Jacqui Thomas
Cover illustration by Doug Sandland
Interior design by Antonia Banyard

Readers are welcome to
contact the authors at
david@davidspalding.com
or via Whitecap Books at
whitecap@whitecap.ca

Printed in Canada

National Library of Canada Cataloguing in Publication Data

Spalding, Andrea.
  The Klondike ring/Andrea Spalding, David Spalding

  (Adventure.net ; #4)
  ISBN 1-55285-461-2

  1. Klondike River Valley (Yukon)—Gold discoveries—Juvenile fiction.
2. Dawson (Yukon)—Juvenile fiction.   I. Spalding, David A. E., 1937–
II. Title.   III. Series: Adventure net ; #4
PS8587.P213K56 2003   jC813'.54   C2003–910247–5
PZ7.S7319Kl 2003

The publisher acknowledges the support of the Canada Council for the Arts and
the Cultural Services Branch of the Government of British Columbia for our
publishing program. We acknowledge the financial support of the Government
of Canada through the Book Publishing Industry Development Program for our
publishing activities.

Note to educators: A Teacher's Guide is available for this book

For Gerri Cook — who kick-started our writing careers and has been a friend, inspiration, and mentor ever since. With love, D and A.

ACKNOWLEDGMENTS

Our thanks go first to Pierre Berton and the committee of Berton House, Dawson, for giving us the opportunity to spend a wonderful three months in the Yukon. Our editor Carolyn Bateman has made many useful suggestions and been a pleasure to work with, while the Whitecap team have been excellent collaborators, as always. Many Dawson residents welcomed us, and assistance particularly relevant to this book came from (in alphabetical order):

Father Tim Coonan (for vehicles, boots, and a theatre box); Jack Fraser and Dawne Mitchell (for a wonderful day panning gold on Hunker Creek); John Gould (who told us the original story of the Klondike ring); Peter Ledwidge and Ann Doyle and their children Marc and Emilie (for insights into their lives as dog mushers); Kathryn Morrison (who gave us a kid's perspective on life in Dawson); Johnny "Caribou" Nunan, Brian Lander, and Bill Willoughby (all most entertaining ghosts of Robert Service); Shirley Pennell (whose dog once towed her bicycle); Freda Roberts, her colleagues, and elders of the Tr'ondek Hwetch'in who gave us insights into the people of the river; Suzanne Saito (Berton House's fairy godmother) and Akio Saito (who used to run the raft race); the Revs. John and Carol Tyrrell (rubber boots, parades, and their enthusiasm for "the Bishop").

CHAPTER ONE

"Half an hour stop for dinner," called the bus driver, pulling into a remote roadside gas station. He punched open the doors.

The expensively dressed young woman from the front seat leaped up and headed outside. Willow, Rick, and the handful of other passengers followed.

"Where are we?" said Rick. He scratched his dark hair with both hands, then rubbed his eyes and stared around. "There's no town. It's just a gas station and hamburger joint in the middle of the Yukon wilderness."

"Maybe there's a village nearby," suggested Willow. "Look, there's a native craft store," she added, pointing to a log cabin in the bushes.

They wandered in and admired the beaded moccasins and mitts.

"Sweet." Willow held up a deer hide vest.

"Forget it; it would take weeks of allowance. Even the dream catchers are $30," said Rick.

"I guess they're more than we can afford," said Willow.

"How about this?" She held a beaded barrette against her fair hair.

"Yeah, right," said Rick. He pointed upwards. "What about that?"

Hanging from the rafters was a beautiful birchbark canoe.

"Dream on," said Willow, laughing.

"Guess you're right. Let's order dinner."

She looked at her watch as they settled at a picnic table. "It's six o'clock. We're about halfway to Dawson City."

"Didn't expect to eat outdoors on this trip," said Rick, adding the fixings to his burger.

"It's June," Willow reminded him. "This is summer, even in the North."

A shrill laugh made them turn toward the takeout window. It was the young woman from the front of the bus.

"If you don't know what a mocha latte is, I guess I'll settle for coffee," she said loudly.

Rick grinned. "Guess she's forgotten we're not in the big city."

Willow nudged him. "Shh, she'll hear." She stared admiringly at the young woman's leather pants. "Dig her gear, though."

"Yeah, yeah," groaned Rick. "Four boring hours to go. Why don't they sell comics or books? We should have taken a plane."

"Mom said it was too expensive. Besides, she thought we might like to see the country between Whitehorse and Dawson City."

8

"Well, that's what we're seeing," said Rick. "Country."

"You haven't seen anything," teased Willow. "You went to sleep in the first ten minutes."

"So what did I miss?" said Rick. He waved his arm. "Trees, trees, and more trees. They're not even big and spectacular like the cedars in B.C." He pointed to the scrubby spruces across the road.

"We're going north," said Willow. "The trees get smaller and smaller. Dad said there are none at the Arctic Circle."

A young couple in matching khaki shorts and jackets stopped talking to each other in German and turned to Rick and Willow.

"You go to the Arctic Circle?" the man said eagerly. "You know how to get there?"

Willow shook her head. "Sorry. We're going to Dawson. Our parents are working there. Dawson's still a few hundred kilometres south of the Arctic Circle. But the tourism people should be able to tell you there."

The German couple thanked them and wandered away.

The young woman from the front seat walked over.

"Hi, mind if I join you? I don't want to sit on a log in these pants."

"Sure." Willow moved up her bench. She glanced at the woman's silk shirt and wished she wasn't wearing an old T-shirt.

"Hi. I'm Kate Van Sacker. I overheard. I'm going to work in Dawson City too. What do your parents do?"

"We're Willow and Rick Forster." Willow performed the

Where would you look for the fifth longest river in North America? Not many people would think of the North. The Yukon River rises in Tagish Lake on the British Columbia–Yukon border, within a few kilometres of the Pacific. Then it flows inland in a great loop, taking 3185 kilometres to reach its outlet on the Bering Sea. In between, it gives its name to the Yukon Territory, Canada's westernmost land area, and flows on through Alaska.

"The Yukon" usually refers to the broad area traditionally accessed from the river in both Canada and the U.S., while "Yukon" refers to the western territory of Canada. It was established in 1898 from part of the old Northwest Territories, when the Klondike gold rush brought thousands of miners from all over the world.

Yukon's first capital was in Dawson, near the Klondike goldfields. After the gold rush declined and the Alaska Highway brought new population and status to Whitehorse, the capital was moved there in 1953.

Around 33,000 people, about 20 percent of whom are First Nations, can call themselves Yukoners. They vote for their own government, which works with a commissioner appointed by the federal government to look after their affairs. The territory gets its money from mining, forestry, and tourism.

www.gov.yk.ca/yukonglance/

10

introductions. "We've come from Vancouver. Mom and Dad are filmmakers."

"They're making a movie about the gold rush and some poet dude for Parks Canada," added Rick.

"Not Robert Service?" said Kate.

"Yup, you know him?" asked Rick.

"Well, since he's dead, I only know of him," said Kate. "You should too. You must know … *There are strange things done in the midnight sun, by the men who moil for gold …*'"

Rick shrugged.

"I'm from Ontario, but I'm going to be with Parks Canada too," Kate continued. "I'm going to be the new special events coordinator," she finished proudly.

"Whatever that means," muttered Rick.

"I'll put on programs to help visitors learn more about the gold rush."

"I thought there already were programs. Mom told us about a historic walk around the old buildings with an interpreter in old-fashioned clothes," said Willow.

Kate nodded. "There are lots of programs." She ticked them off on her fingers. "A walk through the town, one along the waterfront, authentic re-creations of historic characters in the commissioner's house, Robert Service's cabin and Jack London's cabin. Then out in the creeks there's tours around a giant dredger and the Bear Creek mining camp. But I'm going to arrange special events. Like Canada Day concerts and events for Discovery Days. I've got big plans for that. I'm going to resurrect the Discovery Day Raft Race."

11

Despite himself, Rick was interested. "What's Discovery Days?" he asked. "And why a raft race?"

"Discovery Days celebrates the discovery of Klondike gold on August 16th, 1896. There's all kinds of events, including a parade, and this year ... my raft race. I want to celebrate how the miners got to Dawson. Most of them climbed the Chilkoot Pass, then built some kind of raft or boat and floated down the Yukon River."

"Sounds fun," said Rick. "Do we get to build our own rafts?"

"Oh, you can't enter," said Kate. "You're too young."

Rick eyed Kate with dislike.

"Ten minutes," shouted their bus driver.

Kate went to get a refill of coffee.

"She's a pain," said Rick. "Did you see she was eating her fries with a fork!"

"Great clothes, though."

Rick made gagging sounds.

They walked back to the small white bus labelled "Dawson Courier." "It's just a converted school bus," said Rick. "But it's not as good as ours."

"Or as comfortable," agreed Willow, thinking longingly of the cozy seats and their tiny bedrooms in the converted school bus her parents had fixed up as "home" for their frequent travels. "We should have driven up with Mom and Dad last week."

"And missed going fishing with Grandad and Grandma? No way," said Rick.

The driver opened the back doors of the bus, and the kids watched as he stowed cartons of eggs delivered by a woman who'd just arrived in a pickup.

They stared into the luggage compartment. Along with the cartons of eggs and boxes, obviously deliveries from Sears catalogue, there were two kayaks with paddles and life vests.

Kate rejoined them, balancing her coffee and waving a paper bag. "Look what I've just found," she crowed and pulled a pair of richly beaded moccasins out of the bag.

Rick's eyes widened. "You bought those?"

Kate nodded. "I couldn't resist. Aren't they beautiful?"

"They're lovely," said Willow. She ran a finger over the beaded flowers on the front.

"If I had money, I'd buy the canoe," Rick said. His eyes lit up and he nudged Willow. "Let's find a whole bunch of gold nuggets, like the gold rush miners. Then I can."

"Most miners didn't find gold," said Kate flatly. "Most found nothing."

"Imagine coming all this way in a gold rush and finding nothing. How awful," said Willow, as she climbed into the bus.

"It was," said Kate, settling into her seat. She turned to Willow. "Yet they remembered the gold rush as the most important experience in their lives. They went back home and wrote books about it, or told stories to their children and grandchildren."

"So they kind of found something important," said Willow thoughtfully. "Just not gold."

Kate nodded. "I guess everyone who travels to the Klondike

13

is looking for something. What are you kids hoping to find?"

Willow chuckled. "Adventures," she responded. "We always have adventures doing crazy things with Mom and Dad."

"Adventures are great, but I want a gold nugget," Rick said defiantly.

He stared at Kate. "What are you looking for?" he asked bluntly.

Kate laughed, embarrassed. "I need gold too, but I'm a hundred years too late," she said. "So I'll settle for big bucks. I'm going to use my knowledge of gold rush history to earn enough money to pay off my bills. I'm broke. In fact, I might have to moonlight and work two jobs. Build up my bank account."

Willow looked at her expensive clothes. "You don't really look broke."

"I guess," answered Kate. "But I've got to have nice clothes for work." She gave a confidential grin and leaned forward. "And a degree costs a lot. I've got a lot of student debt … and a widowed mother."

Rick's eyes dropped to the expensive moccasins. He stifled a grin.

"Time to go," shouted the driver and started the engine.

Rick plugged his ears. "That engine needs a tune-up. It's too noisy to talk." He took out his portable CD player, stuck in the earplugs and began to twitch his foot.

Willow sighed and pulled out her book. I wonder what Mom and Dad are doing? she thought.

Marty Forster and Shari Jennings, Rick and Willow's parents, stood in the middle of Dawson staring with admiration at the Palace Grand Theatre.

"What character these old buildings have," said Shari. "They're far more interesting than modern ones."

Tall and narrow, the false-fronted wooden theatre, complete with second-floor balcony, was an accurate reconstruction of the original theatre that had stood on the spot in gold rush times.

They entered the foyer, with its old theatre posters and big black wood stove.

"We'd need a crowd in here to bring it to life," said Marty.

"That's easy, there's a play on every night," Shari said, scribbling in her notebook.

Marty extended his arm in a gesture of old-fashioned courtesy. "May I escort you to your seat, Madame?"

Shari lifted the skirt of an imaginary long dress and took his arm. Together they pushed open the swing doors to the auditorium.

"Magnificent," she breathed.

A riot of colour met their eyes: red plush curtains; a gold-framed stage; red, white, and blue bunting hanging from tier upon tier of curtained boxes; a polished wooden floor and rows of black wooden chairs facing the stage.

Shari chuckled. "Makes me wish I was really a Klondike belle," she said.

"You'd need a new hairdo as well as new clothes," said Marty, smiling. "Your current style might have caused comment a century ago."

Shari's hand went up to her short spiky red hair. "I guess you're right. So how are we going to use this wonderful place? It deserves more than a few passing shots."

"We can't film the play," said Marty. "Even if they'd let us, it's nothing to do with Service."

Shari nodded, "Can't you see the theatre as the setting for a Victorian concert, and someone reciting a Service poem?" She ran down to the front of the auditorium and up the steps to the stage. Standing before the red velvet curtains, she clasped her hands to her chest and declaimed, "*A bunch of the boys were whooping it up in the Malamute saloon.*"

"*The kid that handles the music box was hitting a jag-time tune,*" Marty's rich voice joined in the ballad.

They both forgot the next line and burst out laughing.

"Didn't we find a historic photo of a community concert," said Shari. "We could reconstruct it."

Marty waggled his finger. "Remember the budget. No money for actors."

"Leave it with me," said Shari. "Parks has a new special events coordinator coming. And we have two kids who are going to be at loose ends all summer. I feel an idea coming on." She pulled out her notebook and scribbled again.

Pete Eriksen drove his front-end loader to the top of the sluice, dumped the load of gravel into the hopper, and backed up the rough track. He wiped his forehead, shut off

16

the motor, and gazed around. It was pleasant up on the sunny hillside. A light breeze kept the mosquitoes down. In the silence, he heard the creek burbling below. He narrowed his blue eyes, squinted into the sunshine, and following the stream's course through heaps of rock and lines of willows down to the Klondike River.

"I'll follow the bottom gravel and hope there's more gold," he muttered to himself. "We're sunk if there isn't!"

He climbed down from his seat in the loader and eye-balled the pile of coarse gravel beside him — about another week's screening before he needed to dig another load out. But he guessed this pile was hopeless. He'd found so little gold it was hardly worth the cost of running the sluicing machine. He scanned the line of the creek again. The untouched gravel appeared and disappeared under a thick layer of black muck. It would take a good month to blast off the muck with a water jet — but he might find some mammoth ivory buried in the dirt. That always brought in good money. Then he'd bulldoze the top gravel to get down to the coarse layer just above bedrock — the pay streak where the gold should be. Pete nodded to himself. If he took advantage of the long hours of daylight, he might just be able to finish it all before frost hit. He hoped so. He'd probably find enough ivory and gold to see his family through the winter, but after that … ?

Pete hiked downhill to his truck. Through the trees he could see the roof of the cabin his grandfather had built near the creek. It was looking pretty ramshackle. Grandfather had built on his claim nearly a century ago, never dreaming that another three generations would work it.

Pete sighed. He would be the last. There was probably not much pay dirt left now and he didn't know how to tell his son Casey, who dreamed of working the claim when he grew up. Yet it was hard to stop — to ignore hope of a big nugget or a rich pocket of gold dust hiding in the next scoop of gravel. The thought of closing down the mine was almost unbearable. Then what would the family do? Life in the Yukon was good. His grandad's friend, Robert Service, had said it best. Pete paused and spoke the words aloud.

"There's gold, and it's haunting and haunting;
It's luring me on as of old;
Yet it isn't the gold that I'm wanting,
So much as just finding the gold.
It's the great, big, broad land 'way up yonder,
It's the forests where silence has lease;
It's the beauty that thrills me with wonder,
It's the stillness that fills me with peace."

Pete stopped and listened to the stillness. He pulled out his handkerchief and blew his nose hard. We're lucky living here, he thought. He squinted up at the sun again. Time to eat my sandwiches, then a few hours' work with the loader before going home.

"What's that up ahead?" Rick asked the bus driver. He

pointed to a distant dark spot moving across the road.

"A bear," said the driver. "We often see her around this stretch. She's got two cubs."

As they got closer, he slowed the bus, and all the passengers were suddenly awake and eager. The German couple mounted telephoto lenses and began shooting through the windows.

The bear paused on the edge of the pavement, her two tiny cubs pressed by her side.

"She's big and light brown. Is she a grizzly?" asked Rick.

The driver chuckled. "Grizzlies are twice her size. You don't want to meet one of those. No, she's what's called a cinnamon. It's a colour variant of the black bear." He snorted. "Bears look nice but they're trouble. You stay away from them."

The bear looked scornfully at the bus and ambled off over the road allowance, her two cubs scrambling at her heels to keep up.

The bus sped up and began to descend a long hill.

"The Klondike River," said the driver, pointing to a wide, fast-moving stream. "The first gold was found up the creeks over the far side."

The passengers gazed down into the mined valley. It was a broad scar through the forest, its floor full of long heaps of gravel and rocks.

"What are those?" asked Rick. "Looks as if huge worms have been eating the whole valley!"

"Not far wrong," answered the driver. "Over the years, pretty well the whole valley has been chewed up and spat out by giant dredgers. But miners still work in holes and corners that got missed. Dawson's the City of Gold, and it's coming right up."

Everyone strained forward as the bus rocked and rolled round a cliff beside the wide Yukon River, and along the front of a huddle of old-fashioned, false-fronted buildings, built on the river flats.

"He called this a city," whispered Willow. "It's tiny."

Rick didn't answer; he was looking for his parents.

They passed a steamboat pulled up on the land and turned into a dusty parking lot. The Dawson Courier pulled in beside the blue Forster-Jennings bus with a large orca and the words "Orca Enterprises" painted on its side.

Shari and Marty stood beside it, waving.

This time Rick and Willow were out of the bus first. They exchanged hugs with their parents.

Kate followed and stood behind them, obviously itching to be introduced.

Rick ignored her, and Willow felt uncomfortable, but felt she had to say something. "Mom, Dad, Kate was on the bus with us," she said quickly, then wandered off to find luggage.

"Oh, Mr. and Mrs. Forester," gushed Kate. "The children told me all about you. You're making a film about Robert Service. I'd love to help out. I'm the new special events coordinator for Parks Canada."

Shari Jennings was just about to correct Kate's use of their names but changed her mind. This young woman might be useful. "Pleased to meet you, Kate," she said. "I'd heard you

The Klondike Gold Rush

In 1896, George Carmack, Dawson Charlie, and Skookum Jim Mason struck it rich on Rabbit Creek, a tributary of the Tr'ondek (Klondike) River. Before the year was out, many other miners had moved to the area and staked claims on Rabbit (now renamed Bonanza) and other creeks in the area. The first miners to get rich headed out by ship.

When they arrived in Seattle and San Francisco, the news flashed round the globe, and the world caught gold fever. An estimated 100,000 people set out for the goldfields, mainly from the U.S., but also from Europe, Australia, and New Zealand. A few reached Dawson that fall, but most had to survive the dreadful northern winter somewhere on the way. The favourite route was by ship up the west coast, where Dyea and Skagway became major supply points. The would-be miners struggled over the Chilkoot Pass or White Pass, built boats and headed down the Yukon River. Some 30,000 made it as far as Dawson, where they found almost no creeks left to stake.

The lucky few took out $100 million in gold in the next eight years. Many headed home; others found work on other people's claims or serving the needs of the many miners in the area until new gold finds in Alaska provided fresh hope of riches.

**http://www.washington.edu/uwired/outreach/cspn/curklon/
main.html**

were coming. When you're settled at the office, we'll get together and talk."

"Oh indeed," Kate said. "I'd love to be in the movie business."

"Don't give up your day job," said Marty. He turned briskly to Rick and Willow. "Let's load up and drive to the campground. It's late. People will want to sleep and the bus is noisy."

"Who'll be sleeping? It's still afternoon," said Rick, gesturing to the bright sun.

"Welcome to the North," said Marty, laughing. "It's nearly eleven o'clock at night."

CHAPTER TWO

Rick and Willow hardly slept. After dozing on the journey, they discovered the summer sun shone almost all night long, and so they tossed and turned for several hours. Next morning Marty had to wake them up and dump them into their seats. Shari thrust bananas into their hands as Marty drove the Orca bus out of the campsite. They munched passively as he took them over a bridge across the Klondike and down the main road to the edge of town.

"Hey, where are we going?" said Rick as Marty turned up a bumpy gravel road.

He scratched his hair till it stood on end and peered through the windshield. Log cabins and brightly painted houses passed slowly by, interspersed with flourishing gardens and empty lots full of trees.

"Down Eighth Avenue of Dawson City," said Shari. "It's nicknamed 'Writer's Row.'"

Rick yawned. "It is! Why?"

Marty pulled up at the roadside.

Shari pointed. "That's Jack London's log cabin, this white

23

house beside us is Pierre Berton's, and the cabin across the road belonged to Robert Service."

"Jack London?" repeated Rick blankly.

"You'll remember when you're awake," chuckled Shari. "You read his book *The Call of the Wild*."

"I remember that book." Willow rubbed her eyes. "It was about a dog." She punched her brother's arm. "You laughed at me because I cried when the dog ran off with the wolves."

Rick grinned. "Oh, that one." He looked around with renewed interest.

Marty pointed to the house beside them. "Pierre Berton used to live there when he was your age. He's written a lot about the history of the Klondike gold rush. You'll remember his kids' book, *The Secret World of Og*."

"Read that one too," said Willow.

Rick nodded in agreement.

"We're working here." Marty pointed across the road.

A tiny log cabin with a sod roof was nestled among the trees. A huge pair of moose antlers rose from its gable. Log steps climbed to the front porch where a slim young man in shirt sleeves, a black vest, and a trilby hat got up from a hammock and waved.

"Who's that?" asked Rick.

"Robert Service's ghost," answered Marty, deadpan.

"Pretty substantial ghost," said Willow.

"His name's Jamie," Shari explained. "He works for Parks Canada and he gives the Robert Service program twice a day. We're going to film the morning session. If you hurry, you can be in the audience."

"Didn't all the guys wear beards in those days?" Rick queried.

"Not if they worked in a bank," said Marty.

While Shari and Marty set up the camera equipment, Willow and Rick threw on some clothes and headed up to the cabin.

Jamie gestured for them to step inside. The room was gloomy, lit only by a tiny window on each side. The kids peered around.

"Like the wood stove," said Rick.

"That's always the most important object in a cabin," said Jamie. "Yukon winters can be 60 degrees below zero."

"Don't log walls keep out the cold?" asked Willow.

"They're okay if they're well chinked," said Jamie. "But the old-timers often added extra wallboard, or even cardboard, and stuffed some kind of insulation behind, like this … " Jamie pulled out a corner of wallboard to show screwed-up newspaper behind it. "Anything to help keep the heat in."

"Is this where Robert Service wrote his poems?" said Willow, touching a small table.

"Some of them," said Jamie. "But he'd already published a book before he arrived in Dawson. Service was working in the Dawson bank when he discovered the royalties from his book brought in more money than his bank manager earned. He quit, rented this cabin, and wrote a novel and more poems."

25

Robert Service

 Robert Service was born in Preston, England, in 1874. He came to Western Canada to live out his dream of the Wild West. After some years wandering, Service was broke and joined a bank in British Columbia.

He was transferred to Whitehorse in 1904, after the gold rush, wrote his first poems using the colourful stories he heard in the North, and recited them at community events. His first book became enormously popular, and he was well known by the time he was transferred to Dawson. He quit the bank and became a full-time writer in his little cabin.

Here he wrote a gold rush novel and more poems, took them to Ontario and New York for publication, and returned to write more. During World War I, he was a war correspondent and ambulance driver and fell in love with France, where he married and lived most of the rest of his life.

Service probably sold more books and earned more money than any other poet of the 20th century. He continued to write and visited Hollywood when his books were filmed.

There are schools named after Service in Dawson, Yukon, and Lancieux France, where he died in 1958.

www.robertwservice.com/index.html

"What's that?" asked Rick, pointing to a crude machine on the table. "A typewriter," said Jamie. He cocked his head on one side and smiled at Rick. "A sort of pre-electronic word processor?"

"Yeah. I know what a typewriter is," said Rick, laughing.

"Okay. But Robert Service only used it for typing out his final draft. He wrote his first drafts by hand. He'd scribble lines from his poems on big sheets of paper and pin them up on the walls, then he'd stride around saying the words out loud, changing them until the lines sounded just right." He glanced out of the doorway. "Oops! My audience is arriving. It's time to start the program."

Jamie rushed out of the cabin and Marty and Shari began filming as he greeted visitors.

Willow nudged Rick as they joined the audience. "The German couple from the bus are here." They waved.

Jamie stood on the lawn. "Good morning, everyone. Welcome to the home of Robert Service. I'm Jamie McFadden, your friendly parks interpreter." Jamie began to tell the story of Robert Service. The audience laughed as he recited the grace that Service had composed at the dinner table at the age of six.

God bless the cakes and bless the jam;
Bless the cheese and the cold boiled ham;
Bless the scones Aunt Jeannie makes,
And save us all from belly-aches.

Jamie described Service's stern upbringing in England and Scotland, and his longing for the freedom of North America. Finally Service found himself working in a bank in Whitehorse. There he heard wonderful stories of life in the North. These inspired Service to write a poem and recite it at a party:

"*A bunch of the boys were whooping it up in the Malamute saloon,*" he began.

"The Shooting of Dan McGrew," whispered the people in front of Willow and Rick. They mouthed the words along with Jamie.

> *The kid that handles the music box was hitting a jag-time tune;*
> *Back of the bar, in a solo game, sat Dangerous Dan McGrew;*
> *And watching his luck was his light-o'-love, the lady that's known as Lou.*

Willow and Rick sat fascinated as Jamie brought to life the dramatic story of "*a miner, fresh from the creeks,*" who stumbled into a bar, bought drinks all round, and pounded out his emotions on the piano, telling of his love for Dangerous Dan McGrew's girlfriend. In a dramatic climax, Jamie roared:

> *… and the lights went out, and two guns blazed in the dark;*
> *And a woman screamed, and the lights went up, and two men lay stiff and stark.*
> *Pitched on his head, and pumped full of lead, was Dangerous Dan McGrew,*
> *While the man from the creeks lay clutched to the breast of the lady that's known as Lou.*

"Yea," yelled Rick, clapping enthusiastically as the rest of the audience hooted and hollered. He turned to Willow. "That was great. It was exciting too. For poetry it wasn't at all bad." He looked around with wonder. "This Robert guy must be really famous. Lots of people know his poems."

Willow laughed. "Not everyone's like you, little brother. Some people like poetry." She got up and stretched. "I wonder if Mom and Dad are finished. I want to explore."

"Me too." Rick stood on the bench and looked for his parents. "We didn't get to see anything of Dawson last night."

They had to wait. Marty was filming the dispersing crowd, and Shari was interviewing the German visitors about what had brought them to Dawson.

Rick passed the time by repeatedly running up and down the steps of the cabin, timing himself on his stopwatch.

"Rick, quit that, you're driving us all nuts," said Shari. She went over to Marty and whispered. "The kids are pretty restless. Why don't we send them downtown for lunch and meet them later?"

Marty nodded as he moved in for a shot of the cabin through overhanging tree branches.

Shari pulled a crumpled $20 bill out of the back pocket of her jeans. "Lunch money," she said firmly. "Not comics, or candy, just lunch. And I want the change back!"

Willow grinned.

"You can't get lost, Dawson's tiny and the restaurants are within a couple of blocks downtown." Shari pointed north along the avenue. "Turn left on Mission and walk straight down to the river, then turn right along Front Street. You'll see several places to eat. If you don't fancy anything else, there's a hamburger joint nearly opposite the *Keno*, the sternwheeler on the waterfront. Meet us by the *Keno* at two o'clock."

Marty pulled Willow to one side before they left. "It's your mom's birthday in a couple of weeks, have you remembered?"

"Oops," said Willow. "Thanks for reminding us."

Marty nodded. "Now would be a good time to check out downtown for a gift. We're off up the creeks tomorrow."

Rick and Willow waved goodbye to Jamie and walked along the gravel road.

Down the hill from Robert Service's cabin, Casey Eriksen tugged down on the peak of his baseball cap, climbed on his bike, and gripped the rope tied on the handlebars. This was the moment of truth. Would Shar Cho be a sled dog with no snow?

He'd spent days planning this stunt. He'd figured out the longest stretch of boardwalk in town — here, in front of the museum — and successfully sneaked out the dog harness and several metres of rope despite his mom coming home unexpectedly for lunch. If she'd spotted it, he might have had some explaining to do, since the last snow had disappeared from town a couple of months ago.

The biggest struggle had been getting Shar Cho harnessed. The big grizzled brown dog wasn't stupid. He knew there was no snow.

"Ready, Shar Cho?" called Casey. He tugged the rope.

The dog twitched his pointed ears and turned to look at Casey, but continued lying on the boardwalk looking as if a brisk run in the hot sun was the last thing he had in mind.

"Hike!" yelled Casey.

Shar Cho looked up and lolled his tongue.

"I mean it," yelled Casey. "Hike, you half-witted four-legged furball."

Reluctantly, Shar Cho climbed to his feet.

Casey yelled again. "HIKE!"

Shar Cho began to stroll along the boardwalk, taking up the slack in the rope. When he felt the pull of Casey and the bike, he stopped and looked around.

Casey tried another tack. He began to pedal gently, beside the dog.

"Come on, boy, let's have a run."

This time, Shar Cho got into the spirit of the thing and began to trot, then run, alongside. Casey gradually stopped pedalling and freewheeled, letting the dog pull ahead and pick up the slack.

"That's it, boy, HIKE," he encouraged.

Soon they were flying along the boardwalk, past the museum steps, bumping over the uneven boards.

"That's it. Let's feel air!" yelled Casey.

Shar Cho picked up speed. Casey grinned. This was nearly as fast as his dog sled. He checked warily for pedestrians. Two kids he didn't recognize were reaching the crossing at

Mission Street, but he could avoid them. Then a movement across the street caught his eye.

"Oh no," he moaned.

A large white husky, Shar Cho's favourite enemy, emerged from a gate.

Shar Cho spotted the other dog. He leapt off the boardwalk and headed across the dusty street. His leap was graceful — Shar Cho landed on all fours and hit the ground running. Casey's fall from the boardwalk was less elegant, with a five-point landing — two knees, two hands, and a nose.

"You okay?" Rick and Willow ran over and helped the boy to his feet. Beneath the lank black hair over his face his nose was bloody. One hand was gashed, his knees were scraped, and there was a dazed look in his piercing blue eyes.

"Gotta get my dog," muttered Casey.

The big grey-brown dog had made it to the middle of the street but was anchored by the rope still attached to the fallen bike. The white husky was circling him slowly, legs stiff and teeth showing.

Growls rumbled in both dogs' throats.

"Shar Cho!" Casey called desperately. "Here."

Both dogs ignored him.

Casey took an unsteady step across the street and tugged on the rope.

Shar Cho lowered his head, looked sideways at the husky, growled rudely, and trotted back toward Casey with his tail held high.

Horses aren't much use in the long northern winters — they can't find grass in deep snow or keep their footing on ice. But dogs can stay alive on meat and fish, can run anywhere on ice or snow that is not too deep, and can sleep curled up in a snowdrift. A whole northern culture has grown up around travel by dog sled. Once essential for winter travel, dog teams are now used for high-energy cross-country races.

Several breeds pull sleds, though most are wolflike huskies. Racing dogs are often not purebred, and different combinations of strength, speed, and endurance are desirable for different races.

Dog racers have to live out of town because they always have more dogs than are allowed within city limits. One dog musher we visited had 27 dogs, plus a number of puppies, and had entered the 1600-kilometre Yukon Quest five times.

Jack London's novels *Call of the Wild* and *White Fang* show dogsledding in Klondike times. But today's racers build high-tech sleds, carry freeze-dried food, and tell their dogs to "Hike" instead of "Mush."

www.everythinghusky.com

The husky yowled an answering threat and ran back through the gate.

All three children heaved a sigh of relief.

Casey sat on the edge of the boardwalk and buried his face in Shar Cho's neck. "Good dog," he whispered shakily. "Good dog."

Rick picked up the bike. Willow untied the rope and handed it to Casey.

Shar Cho rubbed against Casey's legs and sat on his foot, head hanging down.

"Look at him," Rick chuckled. "Your dog's smart. He knows he did something wrong."

Casey gave a lopsided grin. "Me too. That's the last time I try mushing on a boardwalk."

"Take this to fix your nose." Willow handed Casey a bunch of tissues from her pocket. "Do you want help to get home?"

Casey blotted his nose. "Naw, thanks. I'm okay," he said. "Besides, no one's there. Mom will be in her store by now."

"Is it downtown? That's where we're headed," said Rick. "I'll push your bike if you like."

"Sure," said Casey. His nose had stopped dripping, so he wiped off his knees and blotted his hand. "I'm Casey. I live here. You're tourists, right?"

"Not really. I'm Rick and she's Willow and we're here 'cause our parents are making a film about Robert Service."

"*The boys in the bar were whooping it up,*" quoted Casey. He started to limp down the road.

Rick's eyes widened. "You know about him?"

Casey grinned. "Are you kidding! Me and everyone else in Dawson. Even my school's called Robert Service School." He turned and looked for his dog. "Shar Cho! Heel."

Shar Cho, who had been sniffing under the edge of the boardwalk, bounded up beside them.

"What is he?" asked Rick, patting the dog. "His tail looks like a husky … but … "

"Sure, he's part husky," said Casey. "But there's some other stuff in there. Mastiff? St. Bernard? Nobody knows for sure."

"I didn't get his name," said Willow.

"Shar Cho," said Casey. "It means 'big bear' in Han."

"Han?" questioned Willow.

"It's a First Nations language. The one the Tr'ondek Hwetch'in speak. My grandma's teaching me some."

"Are you Tron … dek Hwitch … Hwitchen?" Willow stumbled over the unfamiliar words.

"Mostly," said Casey, deadpan. "But my blue eyes and left leg are Norwegian, and my right elbow is American."

"Come again?" said Rick.

Casey laughed. "My great-grandpa was an American miner who came up to mine in the gold rush," he explained. "He married into the Tr'ondek Hwetch'in. Then my grandma was born." Casey turned and pointed back up the road. "She lives in that senior citizens' home opposite the museum. She married a Norwegian who came out to mine for gold and their son is my dad. Pete. He married my Mom and she's Tr'ondek Hwetch'in, too."

"So what's with the left leg stuff?" asked Rick.

35

The People of the River

When the gold rush reached Dawson, First Nations had been resident in the area for perhaps thousands of years. Skilled caribou hunters and salmon fishers, the people were known as the Tr'ondek Hwetch'in — the people of the river later known as "Klondike."

First Nations travelled widely, seeking scarce resources. In summer they fished for salmon; in fall they hunted and trapped caribou that migrated through the area. They made canoes and lived in huts and houses of several different kinds.

Early miners often married native wives, and some lived with their wider families. When gold seekers arrived in huge numbers, the effect on the Tr'ondek Hwetch'in was devastating. Miners competed for food, mined their hunting areas, and introduced alcohol and diseases. The people moved downriver to another traditional camping area now known as Moosehide. Now most of the Tr'ondek Hwetch'in live in the town of Dawson, but Moosehide is still the site of a First Nations gathering every other year.

An overall treaty was agreed in 1993, and the Tr'ondek Hwetch'in now have several thriving businesses, a strong role in park and game management, and a fine centre interpreting their culture on Dawson's waterfront.

www.yesnet.yk.ca/schools/robertservice/firstpeoples.html

"That's what my grandma said when I asked her to explain my ancestors. It's like a lot of families in Dawson, all mixed up. Say, where are you going downtown?"

"To eat, and to look for a birthday present for our mom," answered Willow. "You said your mom has a store. What does she sell?"

"Not much," said Casey. "Just gold nuggets, jewellery, and mammoth ivory carvings."

"Gold nuggets!" said Rick, eyes wide. "Where from?"

"Dad's gold mine," said Casey.

CHAPTER THREE

"I've never seen a town like this," said Willow as they walked through downtown. "It's like a movie set." She eyed the raised wooden boardwalk that dipped and tilted at crazy angles, and stared around at the wooden buildings, some plain, some with balconies and turrets. Many were freshly painted, but others had hardly seen a paintbrush since the gold rush. Some buildings were shuttered, with windows boarded up, and looked as if they would fall down if the wind blew.

"I reckon those two are leaning together to hold each other up," said Rick, pointing.

"Why are the buildings so crooked?" asked Willow.

"Permafrost," Casey said. "There's ice in the ground underneath. The buildings were put up straight, but when people lit fires inside the ice melted under the foundations and some parts sank." He laughed, and exaggerated his limp as he walked. "Everything in town tilts. Even me."

They zigzagged to downtown, looking at bits of unfamiliar machinery and old tools that decorated many of the front yards.

Casey led the way to a tiny wooden building with an ornate veranda.

He tied Shar Cho to the steps. "Come and meet Mom."

Rick leaned Casey's bike against the balustrade, and he and Willow climbed up and followed Casey into the small shop.

"Mom," Casey called. "I've brought some friends."

A woman with long dark hair came through a curtain. Gold nuggets gleamed in her ears and a large one hung as a pendant around her neck.

"Casey! What you been doing? Look at your nose."

Casey fingered the sore tip.

"Don't touch it," said Mrs. Eriksen. "Come and wash. You need a boo-boo strip on that."

Rick laughed as Casey crossed his eyes.

"You and that dog been up to something stupid?" said Mrs. Eriksen as she ushered Casey behind the curtain. She glanced over her shoulder at Rick and Willow. "Please look around. I'll be back in a minute."

Leaning against the wall was a cracked, curved tusk, nearly two metres long and thicker than Rick's leg. It caught Rick's eye. "Willow, look at this," he said, stroking it gently. "Know what it is?"

Willow looked up from the glass case in the middle of the shop. "An elephant tusk?"

Rick shook his head. "A mammoth tusk. I've seen them in museums." He ran his hand over it again.

"Great," Willow said. "But we're looking for something for Mom's birthday. You'd have trouble wrapping that. Come and see these gold nuggets."

"Wow." Rick stared admiringly at lumps of gold displayed in small dishes around a map of the goldfields in Dawson. Some nuggets were smaller than his pinkie fingernail, others as big as his thumb. They all gleamed richly, but their shapes varied. Some were like tiny round pebbles, others rough blobs or long and narrow. Each had a label — Hunker Creek, Eldorado Creek, Gold Bottom Creek, Bonanza Creek.

"Look, they're named for the places they were found," said Willow, examining the map in the centre of the case. "See, there's Bonanza Creek on the map — Dad says we're going up there."

Suddenly finding gold became very real to them.

Rick pointed to one of the large nuggets. "Imagine finding that in a stream."

Willow nodded. "Let's try."

They grinned at each other.

The phone rang and Casey's mom emerged from the back room to answer it.

"Have you seen the nugget jewellery she's wearing?" Willow whispered. "What if we got Mom stud earrings like those?"

Rick only nodded. He was staring dreamily at the enormous nugget hanging around Mrs. Eriksen's neck.

"Sorry to be so long." She put down the phone and spoke to them. "I'm Lana Eriksen. Casey said you picked him up when that silly dog pulled his bike over."

"It could have happened to anyone," said Rick, knowing it could certainly have happened to him.

"Well, thanks, anyway," Lana said. "Now, what can I do for you?"

"Could you tell us how much earrings like yours are?" asked Willow. "We're looking for a birthday present for our mom."

"About ninety-five dollars for these," she said. "Depends on the exact weight of gold."

Willow gulped.

"Nearly a hundred dollars. They're not very big," said Rick. His face mirrored his shock.

Lana looked at their faces and smiled. "I'll happily give you 10 percent off for helping Casey, but I suspect gold nuggets are too expensive for you, eh?"

Rick and Willow nodded. "Can we talk to our dad about it?" asked Willow.

"Surely," Lana said. "Come back any time."

Casey emerged with a large Band-aid on his nose.

Rick smirked, and Casey flushed with embarrassment. "Don't you dare say anything," he growled. "Mom says I've got to keep it on."

"Let's go for lunch," said Willow. "We have to meet our mom and dad in an hour. Want to come?"

Casey's eyes lit up. He looked hopefully at his mom.

"Okay. I can take a hint," Lana said, popping the till and passing him a ten-dollar bill. "Be back in an hour to watch the store though. I've promised to visit grandma."

Casey gave her a thumbs-up.

Gold is a metal. It is found in stream gravel as flakes (tiny flat pieces) or nuggets (larger chunks). It is also found in solid rock, usually in veins of quartz. It has a beautiful colour and can be worked easily, since it can be melted, hammered, and cast. Since gold does not decay, many ancient objects made of gold have survived in tombs and other hiding places.

In the Yukon, gold is often used in its natural form. Nuggets are prized for their interesting shapes and used to make or decorate earrings, necklaces, pendants, and other jewellery. Most gold is refined (separated from various impurities like silver), and cast into gold bricks. These are very heavy but are easily transported and may be stacked in a bank vault as an investment. Some coins used to be made of gold, and it has many practical as well as decorative uses. Gold leaf is a finely hammered sheet that may be used to cover surfaces and make them shine as if they were solid gold.

www.gold.org

The three children waited on the corner to cross the road while the driver of a large RV tried to make up his mind which way to go.

"What's a gravestone doing in the middle of the side-walk?" asked Rick, giving it a kick.

"Oh, that." Casey grinned. "It's a memorial to the missing toes."

Willow and Rick looked puzzled. "What missing toes?" Willow asked.

Casey waved an arm at the building behind him. "This hotel serves sourtoe cocktails. It's a drink with a real mummified miner's toe in it. One that's been cut off."

"Gross," said Willow. "Why? Whose toe is it?"

Casey shrugged. "It started as a dare. Someone found a pickled toe and kept it to show to his friends. He put it in a drink and dared someone to drink it. Since then thousands of people have done it."

"Yuck, how gross can you get?" gurgled Rick.

Casey laughed and made gagging gestures.

"No way," said Willow, looking pale.

"It's true," protested Casey.

"So why the gravestone?"

"Cause over the years they've had accidents, and some toes got lost," Casey explained. "See. Somebody fell off his chair while he was drinking and swallowed one. One got lost, and one got stolen. The hotel's always on the lookout for spare toes. So if you get to stay around long enough to get frostbite … "

"Or get too close to a chainsaw," said Rick.

"Or slice one off with the lawn mower," laughed Casey.

"Or lose one falling off the boardwalk," interrupted Rick, laughing hysterically.

"I'm going for lunch," said Willow. Her mouth set in a straight line, she marched off across the road, leaving Casey and Rick leaning over the gravestone holding their sides.

Burgers were soon found and eaten. Willow, Rick, and Casey moved on to the ice cream store for dessert.

"Your mom sure has nice jewellery," said Willow in between licks of a rocky road and double chocolate mint cone. "Does she make it herself?"

"Yeah, didn't you see her workbench in the corner of the store?" said Casey, working his way through a triple cone of bubble gum, Smarties, and cookie dough.

Rick nodded. He was too busy with licorice and tiger's tail to answer.

Willow paused. "We need a birthday present for Mom soon," she said. "Nugget earrings would be neat, but we don't have enough money even for studs."

Casey licked his ice cream thoughtfully for a moment. "Get gold pans and find your own nuggets," he said.

"Where?" said Rick.

"How?" added Willow.

"Geez, it's easy. I can show you. Junior gold panning champion, that's me." Casey bit the bottom off his cone and noisily sucked ice cream through the hole.

"Really?" Rick was impressed. "Where do we get gold pans?"

"The hardware store sells them, but I've got loads," Casey said. "I've been panning for years. I have to help in the store this afternoon. But what are you doing after supper?"

Willow shrugged. "Dunno. Mom and Dad didn't say."

Casey pointed across the road to the old sternwheeler beside the river. "Meet me in front of the *Keno* and I'll teach you to gold pan."

"Great," said Rick. "We'll leave a message at the store if anything changes."

The Orca Enterprises bus cruised slowly past.

Rick waved to attract his parents' attention. "Hey, we can check if it's okay right now."

CHAPTER FOUR

"Remember when we were searching for the silver boulder?" said Rick as they waited for Casey that evening. "And we went adrift on a sternwheeler like this one." He swung on the chain across the *Keno's* gangplank.

Willow grinned. She pointed to the large dike holding back the Yukon River. "No way this boat could drift away in a storm like the *Moyie* did. Oh boy, that was scary, but it was a great adventure." She stared around at sleepy Dawson and the peaceful river. "I wonder if anything interesting ever happens here."

"Here comes trouble for a start," laughed Rick, as Shar Cho bounded round a corner, tail wagging.

"What's he carrying?" said Willow.

The dog had bulky panniers strapped onto his back. Casey followed close behind, a shovel over his shoulder.

"Like my work dog?" said Casey proudly. "He's my lead sled dog in the winter, so I give him lots of exercise in summer. It keeps him fit. Otherwise he just sleeps in the sun and puts on weight. Except when I train him to do tricks."

Shar Cho leaped up to lick Willow's and Rick's faces, then trotted obediently at Casey's heels.

"Where are we going?" asked Rick.

"Not far." Casey led the way along the top of the dike between Front Street and the wide brown Yukon River. When he reached the junction where another river joined it, he disappeared, pushing through bushes and sliding down the bank to the water's edge.

Rick and Willow followed.

"This is the Klondike River," said Casey, pointing to the clear, fast-flowing water. "It runs past your campground. It's named after me."

"Get away!" laughed Rick, punching him on the arm.

"Honestly," said Casey, then he grinned. "Well, kind of. It was really called the Tr'ondek and I'm Tr'ondek Hwetch'in, but the miners couldn't say Tr'ondek, so it became Klondike … get it?"

"Tr'ondek … Klondike." Rick and Willow rolled the words around on their tongues.

"Is this the river where they have the raft race?" asked Rick.

"Yeah, but the start is a couple of miles upstream," said Casey. "It finishes here."

"I wish we could be in it," said Rick.

"Me too," said Casey, "but grown-ups think it's too dangerous for kids. Come on. Let's pan for gold." He unpacked three gold pans and a pair of rubber boots from Shar Cho's packs.

Willow looked at the steep bank behind her. "Is there gold hidden in the dike? How come no one from town is mining it?"

Casey grinned as he pulled on rubber boots. "Naw, the bank would have been torn apart by now. We have to go out to the goldfields to find the real gold concentrations."

Casey picked up a shovel and stepped into the water. "Who's going to hold the pan?"

Rick rushed down to the water's edge and held it out.

"There's a chance of gold here, 'cause all the gravel on the river bottom has washed down from the goldfield creeks," said Casey. "So it's a good place to learn panning." He plunged the spade into the river bed and brought it up dripping and full of gravel. He dumped it into the pan.

"No more, this is heavy." Rick waved away another spade full.

Casey waded back to the shore, took the pan and squatted beside the stream.

"Mix in water," he instructed, dipping the edge of the pan in the stream, then churning the contents with both hands. "Then you swish and dip and let the top layers wash away."

Rick and Willow watched as Casey held the pan at an angle, dipping and swirling it in the stream. Fine gravel and silt slid off.

"Keep swishing," continued Casey, pitching out some of the bigger rocks, "until you have small stuff left on the bottom. Gold's real heavy so it won't wash out of the pan."

He swished and dipped some more.

"You've thrown everything away," protested Rick.

Casey shrugged. "So? It's not gold."

"How do you know?" asked Willow.

Casey laughed, "Believe me, it was just rock. There's no mistaking gold."

Willow and Rick watched with disbelief. There was hardly anything left in Casey's pan, just a layer of fine sand.

"Let's peek." Casey swirled the sand in a circle. He stared into the pan. "Hey, we're in luck!"

Willow and Rick peered over his shoulder. Sure enough, a few tiny yellow specks glistened in the sunlight.

"That's what the miners call 'finding colour,'" said Casey, sounding pleased.

"Neat," said Willow.

"That's gold?" Rick's voice was full of disappointment.

Casey elbowed his ribs. "Thought you would find a nugget first try? Naw … you'll have to do a lot more panning than this. Or find enough dust that you can buy a couple. That's what miners do. Get enough of this stuff and it's worth real money." Casey picked up the specks on his finger tip, and dropped them into a little glass vial full of water he pulled out of his pocket.

Rick jutted his chin. "I'm panning till I find a nugget even if it takes all night."

Casey rolled his eyes. "All summer, more likely."

Willow picked up a pan. "Let's try."

Casey sat on the bank and chatted while Rick and Willow worked. He pointed across the Klondike River. "My people

The most important piece of equipment owned by a gold prospector, a person looking for gold, is a gold pan. Like a deep frying pan without a handle, it is easy to carry but allows a sample of gravel to be washed to see how much gold it contains.

Gold is 19 times heavier than water, and that's a lot heavier than any of the rocks in the gravel. A load of gravel is sorted in the pan, using stream water to wash off lighter material, leaving the gold behind — if there is any.

When he's looking for a gold deposit, a prospector heads upstream and keeps trying a sample pan. If he finds any colour — that's fine gold — he'll keep moving upstream hoping to find a richer source. If he finds less in the main channel, he'll try a side stream in case the gold is being washed in from that direction. If he finds enough, he'll stake the ground and try mining, or sell his claim.

The pan can be used in actual mining too, but it is slow if large quantities of gravel have to be worked. All the larger tools of gold mining — rockers, sluices, and even the giant dredges — are just elaborations of the miner's pan. And in the North, anyone can still buy a gold pan in a hardware store and go out and try his luck.

http://2getgold.com/prospecting/technique.htm

had a fishing camp over there. Then thousands of miners floated down from Whitehorse and took over the whole area. That side became a town called Klondike City, except everyone called it Lousetown."

"Yuck," said Willow with a shiver. "Just hearing that makes me itch!"

Casey eyed her wickedly. "Yeah, no running water once the river froze ... cooties in everyone's hair...."

"Stop it," laughed Willow, putting her pan on the beach. She scratched her scalp and shook her long blonde ponytail. "Suggestions like that drive me mad."

"Bed bugs?" questioned Rick.

"Definitely. Millions of 'em," agreed Casey.

Willow scratched all over her body, then stuck her fingers in her ears and sang "Old MacDonald had a farm" at the top of her voice until they quit teasing her and she could start panning again.

Casey picked up a rock and tried to pitch it to the far bank. "There used to be a bridge here," he said, "between Dawson and Lousetown, but the ice swept it away."

"What happened to your people when the miners came?" asked Willow suddenly. "Did they move?"

Casey shrugged. "Yup, why would they stay in Lousetown? They moved downriver to Moosehide where they could fish in peace."

Casey wandered off through the bushes with Shar Cho, and Rick and Willow could hear him trying to teach Shar Cho a

51

trick. Rick listened with half an ear to Casey calling repeatedly "Stick, Shar Cho. Fetch the stick." He would normally have gone to help, but he and Willow were so determined to find gold that they were washing pan after pan.

Rick finally stood and stretched his back with a groan. "This is hard work, and I've only found three more tiny flakes." He sounded discouraged.

Willow flicked back her ponytail and wiped her cheeks, smearing one with mud. "Guess we're not being very smart. We should save our energy for the real goldfields. People have probably been checking this spot for years!"

Rick nodded. "I need to stretch." He dropped his pan by Shar Cho's pack. "I'm going to find Casey. I want to know if we're sourdoughs now we've been gold panning."

"I'll finish this pan," said Willow and hunkered back down by the water.

Dip and swish, dip and swish. She was fascinated by the process and imagined how she would feel if she saw a gleam of gold among the gravel. Somehow this pan felt special. What if I find a nugget? Boy, will Rick be mad, she thought. She continued patiently panning.

Now there was just a thin layer of gravel and sand left in the bottom of the pan. She swirled it. A sudden gleam startled her. "I must be imagining it," she muttered. "Surely I haven't really found a nugget." She remembered being fooled by iron pyrites — fool's gold — in the Kootenays.

Willow dipped and swished some more as Rick and Casey crashed back through the bushes. Casey was explaining that

Gold rush talk is full of special words. Miners referred to each other as *sourdoughs* and *cheechakos*; gold was found as *flour*, *flakes*, and *nuggets*. The best deposits had a *pay streak*, and the law required that miners made a *claim*. Here's the meaning of a few of these special words.

Cheechako — A newcomer to the North.

Claim — A piece of ground legally registered by a miner, who has the exclusive right to dig for gold there. A claim was measured along the length of a creek and was 500 feet (152 metres) long. The first claim on a particular creek is known as the Discovery Claim and is twice the size of a regular one. Other claims are numbered 1, 2, 3, and so on, above or below Discovery.

Flour gold — Very fine-grained gold dust.

Flakes — Very small, flat pieces of gold.

Nuggets — Bigger chunks of gold, sometimes showing crystal structure, and usually rounded by water erosion.

Pay dirt – Gravel containing gold.

Pay streak — A concentration of gold in a placer mine.

Sourdough — A miner who has wintered in the North. The name comes from the sourdough starter that was used to bake bread when no yeast was available. Experienced miners took their supply inside their sleeping bags in cold weather, as the starter dies if it gets frozen.

a sourdough was someone who'd spent the winter in the North, and Rick and Willow were still cheechakos. But Willow didn't pay much attention, for there it was again — a gleam among the pebbles.

"Any colour?" said Casey, as he and Rick peered over her shoulders.

"You're not going to believe this," said Willow. She reached into the pan and pulled out a nugget the size of her fingernail. It was attached to a golden ring.

"Jeez. Where did that come from?" gasped Rick.

"Guess someone lost it," said Willow. "Maybe they were panning like us."

"You lucky dude!" said Rick enviously.

Casey picked the ring out of Willow's palm and examined it. "It's not a modern ring. Looks real old to me. Look at the way the nugget is set in little claws. No one makes rings like that now. Ask my mom."

Willow slipped the ring on her finger and held out her hand. "Wow, looks great."

"You can't keep it," said Rick. "What if it's stolen?"

"Then why would it be in the river?" asked Willow.

Rick shrugged impatiently. "Who cares. Anyway, it's not yours so you should find out who lost it," he snapped.

"You're just jealous," Willow retorted. She slipped the ring into her pocket.

"If it's old, you might be able to keep it. If no one claims it," Casey offered, then stared in surprise as Rick stomped off up the bank in a huff.

Casey and Shar Cho walked back with Willow, while Rick stalked silently ahead. Willow slipped the ring back on her finger and couldn't resist admiring it every few minutes. This is my special ring, she thought — my Klondike ring.

Suddenly Rick turned. "Where do we find the Mounties?" he asked.

"Why?" snapped Willow.

"Because that ring's lost property," said Rick. "You'll have to report it."

"I don't think the Mounties would bother about it," said Casey. "If we'd found it on the sidewalk, maybe. But it's a really old ring. I reckon it's been in the river for years and years. Why don't you put up a notice in the post office. That's what Dawson people do when they find lost things. Everyone goes to the post office to pick up mail and we always check out the notices." Casey scrawled an imaginary notice in the air with his finger. "Found in the river, a nugget ring. Phone blah blah blah and give complete description to claim it." Casey grinned. "See? That gives nothing away, and the ring is so unusual no one is going to get the description right unless it really is theirs."

"Brilliant," said Willow. Her eyes sparkled. "That's what we'll do. I'll keep it safe ... and if no one claims it ... " She paused and looked at her brother. "I'll give it to Mom for her birthday. Okay?"

Rick shuffled his feet. "I suppose," he muttered. "But if you're going to give out our cellphone number, you'll have to tell Mom and Dad. What if they answer the call?"

55

"You're right. That wouldn't work," said Willow. "So how do we do it?"

"Use my home number," suggested Casey. "Mom won't mind. We even have a message machine."

"Great," said Willow. She turned to Rick. "Happy now?"

Rick just nodded. He was not happy. Willow had not only found a nugget but was being really snooty about it. He was determined to try panning again and find a nugget of his own — or something equally as good.

CHAPTER FIVE

"I saw your friend Kate yesterday," said Shari over breakfast.

"She's not my friend," said Rick, his mouth full.

"I think she's kind of cool," said Willow. "I like her neat clothes, but it's kind of exciting what she's doing, too. I mean, leaving home and going miles away to the other side of the country all on her own to do an interesting job."

"She's certainly getting things moving," said Shari. "She was telling me about all her schemes for this summer — lots of good stuff for us to build into the movie."

"Did she talk about the raft race?" said Rick, interested in spite of himself.

"The raft race, the parade, a concert in the theatre," Shari elaborated. "Lots of neat ideas. And she understood what we were doing and had some good suggestions for us." She turned to Marty. "I know you teased her about not giving up her day job, but I think she's really interested in being involved in movies."

Marty clutched his brow in mock agony. "This business

has to make enough to keep the wolf from the door before we can take on a partner," he said.

"Silly," said Shari. "You know that's not what I meant." She turned to the children. "Anyway, she's got something to ask you — but she'll be up at the dredge this morning, so she can ask you herself."

It was gloriously sunny as the family bus drove up the Bonanza Creek road later in the morning. Rick and Willow sat up front for the best view.

"This is the most famous goldfield in the world," said Marty as he steered through the narrow valley. It was forested up steep sides, but the gravel road writhed through a turmoil of gravel heaps, rock piles, and stagnant pools filling the bottom.

"I don't see any mine shafts," said Willow, watching a bulldozer pushing a heap of gravel.

"These aren't deep underground mines," explained Shari. "They're shallow placer mines. Most of the gold is found in the gravel of old stream beds."

Rick nodded. "Casey told us to look in the stream beds." He and Willow exchanged knowing looks. Willow surreptitiously fingered the ring in her pocket.

"The first gold was panned on the surface when this valley was called Rabbit Creek," said Marty. "But the strikes were so rich the miners changed its name to Bonanza Creek."

"They were tough, those miners," added Shari. "They worked right through the winter, lighting fires to melt the frozen ground. Then they scraped out the softened gravel, filling buckets and heaving them up. When they reached bedrock, they stockpiled the gold-bearing gravel for spring. Once the streams were flowing, they could wash it and see if there was any gold."

"What if there wasn't?" asked Rick.

"Then they'd worked all winter for nothing," said Shari. "But there weren't many barren claims here. Hundreds of millions of dollars' worth of gold were taken out of Bonanza Creek."

"So Kate was wrong," crowed Rick. "She said most of the miners found nothing."

"Ah, she's talking about the miners who came over the Chilkoot Trail in what became known as the gold rush," said Marty. "The gold-bearing ground was nearly all staked by people already living up here. It was a year later by the time the rest of the world heard about it. Most of the thirty thousand miners who came from outside got here too late."

"What about the giant worm burrows," said Rick, pointing to the neatly arranged rock piles. "They weren't made by panning for gold."

"Those were made by the dredges. They were brought in years later, to chew up the valley after it had already been turned over by hand. To get the gold the first miners couldn't reach with hand tools."

The bus climbed a hill, and the family looked down on what seemed to be a huge building with great arms pushing out in front and behind.

"That's your worm, Dredge #4," said Marty.

While their parents discussed filming plans with the Parks staff, Rick and Willow toured the dredger. They wandered through the cavernous interior, gaping at the gigantic machinery that had powered the enormous bucket line to scoop up gravel.

"It must have been really noisy," said Willow, surveying the trommel, a giant steel barrel that had revolved and dropped gravel through holes of different sizes.

They leaned through an open window to gaze down at the pond far below, in which the dredge had once floated. Then they stared out of the back, along the tailings stacker. They could see how it had spewed the waste rock that created the long wormlike tailing piles.

They descended the long stairs in the gloom. As they approached the big door, a figure was silhouetted in the bright sunlight ahead of them.

"There you are," sang out a familiar voice. "Your folks said you were in here. Got a minute?"

Rick groaned softly.

"Guess so," said Willow, digging her elbow in Rick's ribs. "What's up?" They joined Kate at the door.

"I need a couple of kids," Kate said. "And your mom said you might be willing to help out."

Rick gave a gusty sigh. "Uh-huh. What with?"

"I'm planning a special concert in the Palace Grand Theatre during Discovery Days. Actually, it was your mom's idea. She's great, isn't she?" gushed Kate.

Dredge #4

The first small dredge was used in the Klondike in 1898, and, eventually, big mining companies bought out individual claims and reworked all the valleys with giant dredges.

Each machine was mounted on a barge and floated in a pond made by damming the stream. The ground ahead was cleared of trees and defrosted by teams of men. Its buckets picked up the gravel, which was run through a 15-metre-long trommel, sorting the pieces into different sizes. Water sluiced the gravel away, leaving the gold in coconut mats. The barren gravel was taken away on a conveyor that dropped it almost 40 metres behind the dredge. Locals remember the rumble and squeak of the dredges being heard several kilometres away.

Dredge #4 is the last complete dredge of more than a dozen once working in the Klondike and was one of the largest ever used. It was built and launched in 1913. Each bucket could carry almost a tonne, as much as three men could shovel in a day. The dredge lifted 540 tonnes of gravel an hour. Every three or four days, around 23 kilograms of gold was cleaned out of the sluices.

Abandoned in 1940, the sunken dredge was taken over by Parks Canada in 1969 as a National Historic Site. It was refloated and moved to a gravel pad and restoration begun. It was opened to the public in 1993, but restoration continues.

http://parkscanada.gc.ca/lhn-nhs/yt/dn4/index_e.asp

Rick and Willow exchanged looks.

"I want to recreate the old-fashioned community concert that was popular in gold rush days."

"Sort of old songs and recitations?" said Willow.

"You got it," said Kate. "I've got adults lined up, but I need some kids. How would you both like to take part?"

"I don't do singing," said Rick.

"I was thinking more of recitations," said Kate. "You could each do something by Robert Service. You'd have a couple of weeks to learn it."

Surprisingly it was Rick who answered first. "You mean like 'The Shooting of Dan McGrew?'"

Kate nodded. "Probably one of the other poems, though. Everyone knows Dan McGrew."

"I might," said Rick. "But what would we have to wear?" he said, suddenly suspicious.

"Ah, yes," said Kate. "I was coming to that. Parks has a costume replica collection from the period. We'd have to see what fits. Meet me in the office later and try some things on. I'll give you the poems too."

"I'm game," said Willow. "It sounds fun. Can I wear a long dress?"

"Essential," said Kate.

"I'm wearing nothing weird or velvet," said Rick firmly.

"Fine," Kate laughed.

As they walked outside toward the office, Rick bent and picked up a rusted pickaxe, with the remains of its shaft broken and weathered.

62

"Hey, look. An old miner must have used this," he said, eyes shining. He turned to Willow. "Think Mom'll let me take it for a souvenir? I know there's not much room in the bus, but if I kept it in my room."

"Hands off, Rick," said Kate sharply. "That's stealing. This is a historic site. Even broken equipment is part of its history."

Embarrassed, Rick let it drop, and Kate walked away.

"She didn't have to be snarky. I don't steal," he whispered to Willow. He kicked a rock. "Wish I'd never said yes to her stupid concert!"

"What did you think of Kate's jeans?" asked Shari, as they reassembled at the bus.

"They'd be hard to ride a horse in," said Willow. "But did you dig the purse?"

"I think it was a Gucci," said Shari.

"Where to now, Dad?" asked Rick, climbing the bus steps.

"We're looking for a claim," said Marty. "Somewhere on the highway before we reach our campground there's a sign saying 'Pete's Paradise' nailed to a fence post. Pete Eriksen said we could film his mining operations, so it's the next place to check out for shots."

"Pete Eriksen … that must be Casey's dad," said Rick, suddenly cheering up. "I'll watch for the sign." He stared eagerly through the windshield.

They were nearly back at the campground before Rick spotted it.

Marty swung the wheel and the bus lurched down a

rough track, wound through a thicket of alder trees, and came to a halt beside the stream.

They walked across a narrow plank bridge and climbed toward a bulldozer working up on the hillside.

A man wearing overalls, big boots, and a tractor cap stopped the machine and leaped out. "Well ... hello there. You must be Marty and Shari." He pumped their hands.

Marty introduced Willow and Rick.

"Are you Casey's dad?" asked Rick.

"I sure am." Pete's blue eyes crinkled when he smiled. "Are you the kids he took gold panning?"

Rick and Willow nodded.

"Well, come and see a real gold mine — though I can't say I'm finding much gold these days." They stepped over long pipes that snaked across bare gravel.

"Giant hosepipes," explained Pete Eriksen. "I wash off the top layers of muck by directing the force of the water on it. It's way faster than digging. Then once the gold-bearing gravel bed is exposed, I use the Cat to scoop it out and pile it beside the sluice." Pete bent and showed how to hold the massive monitor. The neck of his shirt was open, and the kids stared at the gold chain that swung out. A large nugget glinted in the sun.

"Is that the biggest nugget you've found?" said Rick.

Pete grinned and held it out so they could see better. "Nope, the second biggest. My wife's got the biggest."

"Oh yes, we've seen it," said Willow. "She was wearing it when we were in the store."

Pete fingered the nugget. "Found these years ago when I

64

was working with my dad." He shook his head. "None of us find nuggets this size very often. The gold beds are almost cleaned out. Only colour and small nuggets are found now."

"Is it okay if Rick and Willow wander around the claim on their own?" asked Marty. "We're going to be discussing camera angles and action for a while. It's pretty boring."

"No problem," said Pete. "Don't touch any machinery and watch out for bears." He kicked some week-old bear scat on the path. "I heard this one was over the hill yesterday. Make lots of noise in case he's back. He's scared of humans so he'll avoid you."

Rick and Willow pushed their way through a thicket of small birches to the stream. They could hear their parents' voices faintly in the distance.

"Hey, Rick," called Willow. "Wait for me. This is freaky. What if the bear's around? The bus driver said bears are trouble." She stared at the bushes on the far side, which seemed to be moving on their own.

Rick stopped and followed her gaze. "That's the breeze, idiot," he said. "Come on. I think I can see the roof of a building through the trees."

Willow gave herself a mental shake and followed him.

They scrambled over decaying logs, rusty pipes, and finally hit a faint trail along the stream.

"Hey, I see steps in the bank," called Willow.

Rick ran up them. "I was right, it's a cabin."

The logs were old, and the roof sagged badly, but while

the cabin wasn't lived in it was obviously in use. The porch was littered with equipment and an old chair had a coffee mug balanced on the arm. The cabin door was propped open to the shadowy interior.

Rick walked toward it.

"We can't go inside," protested Willow. "It's private. It belongs to Casey's dad." A rustling in the bushes and the snapping of a falling branch made her look round nervously. "What was that?"

"Jeez, you're jumpy today," said Rick. "What's up? We've explored the forest before!"

"Not when bears are around," said Willow. She stared into the bushes.

Rick laughed. "There's no bear. Mr. Eriksen said he was over the hill. Besides, we've been talking all the time. It won't come near us."

Willow was unconvinced. "I feel as though eyes are watching me from the forest." She checked around again and gave a shiver. "I'm going back to the bus," she said. "I can see the bridge, just downstream. Coming?"

Rick shook his head. "I'll hike back uphill and see what Mom and Dad are doing."

Willow looked fearfully around at the trees and bushes. She slipped on the nugget ring for good luck. "Keep bears away," she whispered to it, then ran singing and shouting at the top of her voice to keep away invisible bears.

"Scaredy-cat," shouted Rick at Willow's retreating back.

A movement among a cluster of alder trees caught his eye.

At fifty paces, he and a bear found themselves staring at each other.

After a few moments, Rick gave a yell, picked up the coffee cup and hurled it toward the surprised animal. The bear lumbered swiftly back into the forest, while Rick bolted into the cabin, slamming the door.

Rick stared through the cabin window, his heart racing. Thank goodness the bear had fled in the opposite direction to Willow.

He leaned against the wall and tried to catch his breath, his eyes wandering around the cabin. He needed to warn his parents — once he was sure the bear had gone.

Rick shivered. It was chilly out of the sunshine. He imagined how cold it must be in winter and noted that the logs were covered over with thin, aging wallboard. Extra insulation, he thought. Like in Robert Service's cabin.

A couple of fry pans hung on nails. Rick grabbed them. He could bang them together to scare the bear and warn everyone else within earshot.

As he lifted a pan down, the nail fell out with a whole corner of rotten board attached.

"Oh, shoot," he muttered. "I'm wrecking the joint."

As he bent to pick it up, several wads of brown paper tumbled out on top of him.

"Oh no. The whole place is coming apart," he wailed in frustration. He picked the paper up and noticed it was covered with words written in pencil.

He peeked through the window again. The bear had paused and was looking back at the cabin. While Rick watched, it turned into the trees not far away.

Better hang on a while before I go out, he thought. It's sticking around. He went back to the papers and took one to the window, smoothing it out.

"*There's many a tale told on the trail, by men who grub for gold,*" he read aloud. "*Neath northern lights, on freezing nights, huddled in cabins cold.* It's a poem," he realized, and picked up the rhythm.

"*They scoff their beans with sourdough bread, then each rolls in his bed,*
And takes his turn to call to mind a feast on which he's fed."

Rick stumbled over the words, for some were faded and others crossed out and replaced by others. Curious, he reached up, pulled more paper from the wall, and laid the sheets out on the table. He found more verses and arranged and rearranged them in an order that made sense.

"This poem's funny," he chuckled. "It's like a Robert Service." He pulled out a notebook from his back pocket, and copied the poem into it. It wasn't until he had finished that he remembered the bear.

Rick stuffed the paper back into the wall and rammed back the board. Picking up the two fry pans, he cautiously opened the door of the cabin. No bear in sight. No movement in the bushes. He clanged and banged the fry pans together on the veranda, then ran down the trail beside the stream to the bus.

The easiest gold to mine is found as particles — flakes and nuggets — that have been washed into rivers and streams. As a stream changes its course, it flows over and through beds of gravel and sand where the gold might hide. Gold stays close to its source, while the streams and rivers move lighter material to the sea. Gold and other heavy minerals are concentrated in the gravels beneath and around the river, and a clever and lucky prospector may find these places.

Getting gold from stream valleys is called placer mining, from a Spanish word for sand bank. Placer miners have to dig pits through the sand and gravel from the stream and its banks until they get down to the hard rock that forms the river valley. The heavy gold is likely to be concentrated just above bedrock. Miners have to dig out the gravel and wash it until only the gold is left.

In southern areas such as B.C.'s Cariboo, placer mining was relatively easy. The Klondikers worked farther north, where water in the ground is permanently frozen. Miners had to light fires in their pits to melt the gravel before it could be dug out. Then they had to wait till summer, when the streams melted, before they could wash the gravel and find out how much gold had been dug out.

www.tbc.gov.bc.ca/culture/schoolnet/cariboo/mining/placer.htm

"Bear alert! Bear alert!" he yelled at the top of his voice.

Willow's startled face peered through the windscreen. She opened the bus doors and Rick shot inside.

"You were right. There was a bear," he said. Willow pounded on the horn to warn his parents and Mr. Eriksen.

CHAPTER SIX

When Willow awoke the morning after the bear incident, she smiled and slipped her hand under her pillow. The lucky nugget ring was still there! After it helped protect her from the bear, she had threaded the ring on a chain so she could wear it around her neck without anyone seeing. She held up the chain. The nugget glowed as it swung in the sun's rays. "You're mine," she whispered. "I found you panning, just like a real gold miner. I hope no one else claims you," she finished, remembering the "found" notice she had given Casey to pin up in the post office the previous day.

She sat up. She'd also told Rick she was going to give the ring to her mother for her birthday if it wasn't claimed, but how could she bear to give it away? Ah well, Mom's birthday was still some time away. Maybe they could come up with another present. She slipped the chain around her neck so the ring could hang down inside her T-shirt.

Grabbing some breakfast cereal in the kitchen, she peeked through the window to see her parents already working with their laptop computers on the picnic table. She waved to them.

"Good morning, honey. Sleep well?" called Shari.

Willow nodded, her mouth full.

"You and Rick are in Dawson two days and your social life is busier than ours," teased her father. He handed a scrap of paper through the open window. "Two phone calls already and it's not even nine a.m."

Willow squinted down at the paper, "Just Kate and Casey. Kate probably wants us to check out costumes for the concert."

Her parents went back to work and Willow finished her cereal in peace, then stuck her head out the window again.

"Is it okay if I use the phone?" Her mother nodded but didn't look up from her computer.

Willow dumped her dish in the sink and picked up the cellphone.

Before she could dial, Rick bounced out of his bedroom and grabbed a banana.

"Don't you ever want anything else for breakfast?" said Willow.

"Nope," said Rick cheerfully. "Unless I'm allowed ice cream." He plopped down at the table. "I've been thinking … that ring … "

Willow fingered the chain.

"If no one claims it, can we both give it to Mom?" he asked.

Willow made her mouth smile, but she felt a knot in her stomach.

"Then you'd owe me big time," she hedged.

Rick chuckled. "So what's new. According to you, I always

owe you!" He caught sight of the paper on the table. "What's this?"

"Casey and Kate both phoned," said Willow. "I was just going to call them back. I bet Kate's phoned about our costumes for the show."

Rick scowled. "She's a jerk."

"She wears great clothes," said Willow.

"So, she's a well-dressed jerk."

"Well, I kind of like her. I want to ask her about her education. I might go into heritage stuff."

Willow swirled her long skirt in front of the mirror. With a "leg of mutton" sleeved blouse and a pair of ankle-high laced boots, she looked as though she had just stepped out of the 1890s.

Rick shuffled impatiently.

Kate handed him big miner's boots, a felt hat and red suspenders. "Do you own a checked shirt?" she asked.

Rick nodded.

"Then wear that on the night, with your own jeans, and you'll do," Kate said.

Rick sighed with relief. He laced on the boots and stuck the hat on his head.

Willow giggled. "What do you think?" she said as they looked in the mirror together.

"Could have been worse," said Rick. He clipped on the suspenders and snapped them.

"Are you both ready?" said Kate. "We have to go down the

What did kids wear a century ago? Many children were brought to the Yukon or were born and grew up there, and they appear in some photographs.

School-age boys dressed much like men. Younger ones wore knee-length knickerbockers with long socks, while older ones wore long pants and jackets in heavy material and dark colours. Men and boys normally wore a cap or hat when out on the street.

Girls normally wore dresses, or skirts and blouses, and hemlines were about mid-calf. Garments were often more ornate than modern clothes, with puffed sleeves and fuller skirts. Outdoor materials were heavy and dark, but more formal dresses were white. Dresses were often covered by pinafores at school. Hair was normally long, worn down over the shoulders with ribbons for younger girls. For an older girl, the day she "put her hair up" at 14 or 15 was an important step in becoming an adult. Outside, older girls wore hats.

Because of the intense winter cold and the rough living conditions of the claims, Klondike photographs occasionally show boys in parkas and girls wearing coveralls or long pants under a skirt — the first hints of modern trends toward adopting indigenous clothing and dressing boys and girls more alike.

www.chicagohs.org/AOTM/Jan98/jan98artifact.html

block to the photo parlour. They've promised to take an old-fashioned sepia photo to promote the show."

"I'm not walking down the street like this," yelped Rick. "People will stare."

"This is Dawson," said Kate. "Everyone dresses up. The Mountie wears a scarlet coat and rides a horse, Robert Service reads twice daily in a vest and trilby, and Parks Canada guides are up and down the streets in long dresses all the day long. So who's going to notice?"

She eyed Rick. His chin still jutted stubbornly.

"We could have an extra print made for your parents," she offered.

Willow nudged him. "Remember Mom's birthday."

Kate and Willow led the way down the boardwalk, while Rick slunk along the road between them and the wall, trying hard to be invisible.

"How did you get into parks and stuff?" Willow asked Kate. "What sort of training do you need?"

"Did arts at high school," said Kate offhand. "Lots of public speaking; class valedictorian, school yearbook, most likely to succeed, that sort of stuff. Then got a degree in history and media. I volunteered at the local museum as a guide at fifteen and managed some of these kinds of projects. The board thought very highly of me."

"Neat," said Willow. "I might go that way myself."

"Really?" said Kate, suddenly taking an interest. "Well, any time you want some advice, I'd be happy to talk to you and your mother."

A busload of tourists drew up beside them, and a crowd of elderly people with name tags and southern accents disembarked.

Willow and Rick had to stop to be photographed — together, separately, in front of this building and that, and with members of the tour group. Rick tried to slink off but was waylaid. His photo was taken at least a dozen times.

"You look so cute," said one smiling lady, handing him a dollar.

Rick was out of his costume within seconds of returning to the office, but Willow changed regretfully — she could get used to this adulation.

"Let's go," Rick muttered and headed for the door.

Kate drove them back to the campsite.

"Oh, I nearly forgot," said Kate, handing them each a big envelope as they got out of the car. "Here are your poems. Learn them for next Friday and we'll have a practice."

She whipped a Palm Pilot out of her pocket like a gun out of a holster and clicked a few buttons.

"Yes, Friday, three o'clock. Make sure you know them perfectly," she said, giving each child a hard look. "I won't have time for hand-holding. Then I'll give you a date for the dress rehearsal. The show's on Discovery Day."

"Sure," said Willow.

Rick rolled his eyes and offered his envelope back. "Maybe it's too much trouble," he said. "It is summer, after all."

Kate looked at him sternly. "You do know it's your mother's idea," she said. "She'd be very disappointed if you don't do your piece. She wants you in the movie, you know."

Rick dropped his arm. "I guess," he said.

"What poems are you doing?" asked Shari, waving to Kate as she drove off in a swirl of dust.

Willow and Rick tore open the envelopes.

"I've got 'The Cremation of Sam McGee,'" said Willow.

"Good choice. It's funny," said Marty. "My dad used to recite it."

Rick stared down at his poem. "Mine's called 'The Spell of the Yukon,' but it's not about magic, and it's not funny." He read a few lines:

I wanted the gold and I sought it;
I scrabbled and mucked like a slave.
Was it famine or scurvy — I fought it;
I hurled my youth into a grave …

He dropped the paper on the table. "It's boring." Rick folded his arms across his chest. "I quit."

"Oh come on, Rick, you can't back out now. You said you'd do it." His mom sounded irritated. She picked up the poem and scanned it. "Hmm … it's quite moving. I bet you'll find this is as big a crowd-pleaser as a funny one. Besides, Sam McGee is well known and the audience will expect some surprises in the program or there's no point in going to the concert."

"I guess," he said, lapsing into thought.

"Hi there!" Casey waved from the trees at the edge of the campground.

Rick waved back.

"Come on over," called Willow.

"I can't," Casey hollered back. He grinned. "There's a toy poodle in the campground. Shar Cho tried to eat the last one he saw."

Shari and Marty looked up and chuckled as Rick and Willow ran over to join him.

The three children walked along the edge of the river that flowed beside the campground.

"The poodle's not really a problem," said Casey as soon as they were out of Marty and Shari's hearing. "I needed to talk to you away from your folks. Got a phone call last night. About the ring."

Willow blenched. She clutched the chain protectively through her T-shirt.

"It was kind of weird, though," continued Casey. "Like the woman didn't really know what it looked like."

"What do you mean?" asked Willow.

"Well, she had this crazy story, but it could be true. And I kinda didn't know what to say."

"So what *did* you say?" said Willow fearfully.

"I told her I was just taking messages, and the person who found it would get back to her."

Willow nodded. She sat on the grass by the stream and stroked Shar Cho. "Okay. Give us the story."

The boys squatted beside her.

"She said she and her boyfriend were walking along the river when he gave it to her. She put it on her finger, and waved her hand around to make the nugget shine, but the ring was too big and it flew off and they couldn't find it. She said because she'd only just got it, she hadn't looked at it close enough to give a proper description."

"I shouldn't have said it was in the river, " said Willow. "Why didn't her boyfriend phone?"

"He's off working on the Alaska pipeline," Casey replied.

There was a long silence.

"It sounds as if it could be true," said Rick, looking sideways at Willow.

Willow didn't answer immediately. She stared at the ground, frowning.

"Didn't she notice if it was a modern ring or an old ring?" she said eventually.

Casey fidgeted uncomfortably. "I kind of blew that bit. She was going on and on about it being her ring and how important it was to get it back and I said it didn't sound like the one you'd found because that was an old ring. Then she jumped in saying that was what was so special about it. It had been her boyfriend's grandmother's. See what I mean? It could be true, but it's kind of weird."

"So what do we do now?" said Rick slowly.

"Who's the woman? Is it someone you know?" asked Willow.

Casey shook his head. "She's working in Dawson for the summer to be near her boyfriend. Her name is Kate Van Sacker."

"KATE!" chorused Willow and Rick.

"She's lying," said Rick flatly. "She's a jerk."

"We don't know she's lying," Willow said uneasily.

"Why would she?" asked Casey.

Rick snorted. "You kidding? We met her on the bus coming up here. I don't trust her. She never said anything about a boyfriend. She said she was broke, but you should see the expensive things she buys. I bet you any money she's seen the chance to pick up a free ring. I bet you it's a scam!"

"How will we know, though?" asked Willow.

Rick and Casey shrugged.

Willow sighed. "Guess I'll have to talk to her." She lapsed into an unhappy silence.

"You doing anything today?" said Casey eventually.

Rick shrugged. "Just hanging out here at camp. Mom and Dad are writing their script. Could take hours."

"Want to hang out with me?"

"Sure," said Rick. "What'll we do?"

Casey grinned, "Make a raft. Dad felled some small trees on the creek, just up there." He pointed upstream. "They'd work great."

"Can he cut trees wherever he likes?" asked Rick.

"Sure. It's our land," said Casey. "Grandad bought up a heap of abandoned claims between here and the Bonanza Creek Road. Our property comes almost to the campground."

"Sweet." Rick jumped up. "Let's ask Mom and Dad. Coming, Willow?"

"Don't say anything about the raft," warned Casey. "Moms hate rafts."

Rick grinned.

"Can we hang out with Casey?" asked Rick. "Explore the creek and stuff."

"What about the bear?" said Shari.

"Aw, he was just a young one. Rick scared him off good with those fry pans," laughed Casey. "Dad checked around this morning and apparently he was off up another creek. Besides, we'll have Shar Cho with us. He'd chase him away, wouldn't you, boy?"

Shar Cho looked up and wagged his plumed tail.

"We won't be far away," added Casey. He pointed. "There's a small creek running along the back of the campground. We'll be up there. If you shout, we'll hear you."

Shari looked at her computer, then at Marty. She rubbed her forehead.

"This script is going to take a while, isn't it?"

Marty agreed.

"So what do you think? Is it safe?"

"Well — if they're not far away and they've got the dog," Marty said slowly, then his face brightened. "Got it! Take the whistles off the life jackets and blow like mad if there's any hint of trouble."

"Brilliant," said Shari. "Okay, you can go."

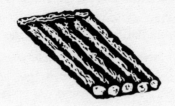

CHAPTER SEVEN

The friends walked along a low bank where tree trunks lay higgledy-piggledy on the ground.

"These were half washed out and leaning dangerously," said Casey. "So Dad's cutting them up for our winter wood."

Rick stared at some of the cut lengths already laid side by side. "That's your raft?"

Casey nodded. "I thought we could make one and then float down this creek."

Rick started toward a small log.

"Hey," said Casey. "The logs need to be fairly big or three of us and a dog won't fit on."

"But not too big and heavy," said Willow. "Or we won't be able to drag the raft into the water."

Rick found a suitable length of log and he and Willow half carried, half rolled it over to the others.

"Got a hammer and nails?" asked Rick.

"Not allowed," explained Casey. He fetched coils of rope from a heap by a tree and pulled out a jackknife from his pocket.

As Rick and Willow watched, he began to tie the logs together, pulling tightly on each knot as he went.

"Hang on," said Willow. "We should make it right beside the water, or we'll have to drag it all the way."

With a grin, Casey unravelled the rope, and they began again.

Rick and Willow bent to help with other lengths of rope.

It was a long hard job.

"Go away," chuckled Willow as Shar Cho sniffed at fingers and licked faces as they bent over.

Eventually, scratched and grazed from rubbing against rough bark, and red-faced from lifting and pulling on logs and ropes, the kids surveyed their handiwork.

Casey leaped up on the raft, stretched out his arms and acted out balancing down a turbulent stream. "Feels good. The ropes are tight," he said, jumping up and down.

Willow's eyes danced. "Let's launch it."

Casey jumped off and the three friends pushed, pulled, heaved, and levered the raft down the bank and into the water.

"Hang onto the rope," called Casey breathlessly.

Rick grabbed the loose end and tied it to a stump.

"Yeah! It's floating," Willow yelled.

The raft bobbed gently up and down in the current.

Shar Cho yodelled with excitement as they pulled the raft against the bank.

Rick leaped onto the logs. One corner dipped into the water, and he staggered and fell to his knees. He waited until the raft stabilized, then rose to his feet. "Taa daa!"

"Hey wait, we need poles," called Casey. He found three straight saplings from the brush pile, handed one to Rick, another to Willow, and jumped on board with the third.

The raft wobbled but stayed afloat.

"Okay, now you join us," he called to Willow.

"Hang on," said Willow. She untied the rope and scrambled on board. The raft visibly sank in the water and a wavelet swept across one corner. The sailors looked apprehensive. Then the raft stabilized again and slipped away from the shore.

It bobbed slowly downstream in the light current, and with practice the friends found they could steer through the shallow water by using the poles.

Sometimes the raft caught on a rock or a gravel bar, and it took much pushing on the poles, and as well as a lot of giggling and jumping up and down to dislodge it.

Shar Cho ran along the bank whining as they floated along, appearing and disappearing behind bushes.

"We're speeding up," said Willow.

"Yeah," said Casey. "The creek's faster and deeper here. We'd better not go round the corner. Hit the bank!"

He and Rick both dropped their poles in on the same side and pushed, forcing the raft toward the bank. As soon as they were close enough, Willow grabbed the rope and leaped into the shallows, pulling hard.

By now, Shar Cho was yowling as if he'd just won the Yukon Quest. The big dog splashed into the water, welcoming them back to dry land.

But Rick's pole had stuck fast. He tugged frantically but couldn't pull it free. He found himself leaning over a widening gap between the pole and the raft. "Help!" he yelled.

The pole came loose, and Rick toppled full length into the water with a gigantic splash.

"It's not funny," Rick sputtered as the other two cackled. "The water's freezing!"

Willow tied the raft to a tree as Casey hauled Rick out of the chest-high water, then splashed downstream to rescue the pole, which was floating near the cabin steps.

By now, both boys were soaking wet.

Rick took off his shirt and squeezed a stream of water out of it. Shar Cho shook himself dry, showering everyone.

"We'd better sneak back for dry clothes without your folks seeing," said Casey. He shivered. "Can you lend me a shirt?"

Rick nodded.

"But better go carefully," said Willow. "Or we'll be banned from rafting for sure."

Shari and Marty were chatting to the neighbours in the adjacent campsite. Shar Cho and Willow appeared and had to be introduced. It took a while for everyone to pat him and for Willow to explain what his name meant.

"Where's Casey ... and Rick?" said Shari, suddenly realizing that the kids weren't all present.

"We're here, Mom," said Rick, stepping out of the bus. Casey followed.

"I was showing Casey my rock collection. We're still going to try and find a gold nugget for it. Oh, and we're real hungry. Can we eat?"

Shari laughed and nodded.

Casey looked out of the corner of his eye at Rick. "Good job your mom didn't notice I was wearing your clothes," he whispered.

Rick grinned. "And a good job the back door was open and we could climb in!"

Willow sat at the table inside the bus staring at the cellphone. She really should have the guts to phone Kate about the nugget ring.

Through the open window she could hear Rick and Casey playing with Shar Cho, and the clatter of the computer keys as her mom and dad resumed working on their film script. Everyone was busy, so now was the perfect time.

Willow lifted the chain from around her neck and stared longingly at the ring. She wanted to own it so desperately, but if it really was Kate's she knew she would have to give it back. With a deep sigh, she spread out the crumpled piece of paper where Casey had scribbled the phone number and picked up the phone.

She put it down again. She should think this through. Rick was convinced that Kate was lying. She wasn't sure, but the story Kate had told Casey was definitely odd. Willow stared at the phone trying to figure out what to say. How could she be sure Kate would tell the truth?

Through the open window, Willow heard her dad's deep voice rumbling a question and her mom answering. Willow grinned. Kate was in awe of her parents. What if … ? She picked up the phone.

"Hi, Kate. It's me, Willow … no, nothing's wrong … no …. of course we haven't lost the poems. I almost know mine." Willow took a deep breath and said in a rush. "It's about the nugget ring. I'm the person who found it."

There was an audible gasp at the other end. "YOU?" said Kate with a brittle laugh. "What a coincidence."

"I could ask my dad to show it to you next time he and mom are in town. You could tell him about your ring and see if it's the same one," said Willow.

There was another brittle laugh at the end of the line. "That won't be necessary," said Kate quickly. "Someone else found mine, but thanks for phoning. I have to go. I'm in a meeting. Bye." The line went dead.

Willow switched off the cellphone and stared at it.

It was early evening. Casey's dad had picked him up on his way home from the mine, and Rick and Willow were washing up after supper. Shari and Marty were taking a walk.

"I asked Dad if I could go on the Net when I've finished," said Rick.

"Okay," said Willow. "But I'd like to go on too when you've done. Why don't I finish your drying so you can get started, and you can do it for me another time."

"Okay," said Rick. "Thanks."

He handed her the towel and booted his laptop, plugged it in to the phone jack and opened up a search engine.

"What are you working on?" asked Willow. "We don't have any schoolwork. It's summer."

"It's a secret," said Rick mysteriously. "Just you wait and see."

"Suit yourself," said Willow. She turned to the drying but kept an eye on Rick. He spent a long time checking between something on screen and something secretive in his note-book. Suddenly he pushed back his chair, yelled "Yes!" and punched the air.

"Found something?" asked Willow.

Rick shut his notebook and logged off. "No, I haven't found anything. That's just what I wanted to find. But I'm not telling you … yet," he grinned. He picked up a ball and went outside.

Willow plugged her laptop into the phone jack, called up a search engine, punched in "Klondike Ring," and scanned the list of sites that appeared.

"Boxing in the Klondike!" she muttered. "— not the sort of ring I'm looking for." She typed "nugget ring" and scanned a series of photographs of modern jewellery with thick bands and elaborate designs.

"Casey was right," she said to herself. "The modern rings are nothing like the one I found. It really is an old ring, old enough no one may claim it."

On impulse, instead of shutting down, she went back to the search engine and punched in a name.

"Kate Van Sacker" turned up in a couple of places. She

was mentioned on a website of a museum in rural Ontario, where she headed a list of volunteers. But there was no other information. She was also on a list of alumni from a college that Willow had never heard of.

"Funny," said Willow as she closed down the Web and clicked the icon for her favourite game. "I don't think colleges give degrees, and I'm sure she said she had a degree."

CHAPTER EIGHT

A whole week's gone by without calls about the Klondike ring, thought Willow, as she sorted laundry in the camp laundromat.

Each morning she'd pulled the ring out and tried it on before dropping the chain under her T-shirt. Each night she rubbed the nugget and made a wish that no one else would phone Casey. So far no one had.

She loved to lie awake in bed thinking about it. It was the most special thing she had ever found, valuable to be sure, and lucky she hoped. But it was much more than that. Because it was found here, in this historic place, it seemed to link her back to past times. No wonder Kate enjoyed her work with history.

Who had found the nugget, she wondered, who had made the ring, and who had owned and worn it? And how had it been lost? Had the nugget been found by a miner on one of the local creeks or brought here from some other gold rush? Was it the work of a local jeweller, or had it been carried away to some great city to be set? And was it given to a sweetheart, a mother, a wife, a daughter? Was it their only jewellery, or was it tossed in a corner of a drawer with dozens of more spectacular pieces? And did it come into the river because someone was careless, or had there been some angry scene, or a wicked crime?

She had stopped pretending to herself she was going to give the ring to her mother, though she hadn't broken it to Rick yet. "Gotta figure out a proper gift for Mom, though," Willow muttered to herself. The photo of us in costume will make a special card, but we have to have a gift." Maybe she could think of something this morning. It was her turn to help with laundry, but it was still early and no one else was using the machines. She loaded up several washers and fed in the quarters. Perhaps she could check something on the computer while she waited for the wash cycle to finish.

"Kate's surname is Dutch," she had said to her mom after breakfast. "If Kate is just a short version of her first name, what might it really be?"

Shari had looked at her daughter, puzzled. "It could be short for a more traditional name. Caterina maybe? Or you could perhaps spell that with a 'K.' Why do you want to know?"

"Oh, just wondered," she said.

But Willow had a reason for asking. She hadn't found much about Kate so far, but if she had another name she might be able to find more stuff.

She opened up the search engine and punched in "Katerina Van Sacker."

"Where's Casey?" Marty drummed his fingers on the steering wheel of the bus and looked again at his watch. "I've got a meeting in ten minutes."

"Dad, you can drive three times round town in ten minutes," said Rick. "But here he comes." Rick had spotted his friend at the end of the street.

"Okay, I'll leave you here then, so you can hang out with Casey. I'll pick you up at the usual place ..."

"The *Keno*?" said Rick.

Marty nodded. "... at the *Keno* at noon."

He backed the bus carefully out of the downtown parking space he'd found and turned up Front Street. He hung out of the window and paused by Casey as he passed.

"Sorry, Mr. Forster," called Casey. "Guess I'm on Yukon time this morning. Who are you meeting?"

"The parks historian," said Marty.

"Hey, relax," said Casey. "Mom was just talking to his wife. He was in Whitehorse for a conference at the weekend and only got back late last night. He'll be late for sure 'cause he'd just poured another cup of coffee so he could wake up properly."

Marty gave a shout of laughter. "It's a small town," he said, shaking his head as he drove off.

Casey turned to Rick. "What did you do with Willow?"

"She's at the laundromat. It's her turn to do the washing — I did it last week," said Rick. "So ... any phone calls?"

Casey shook his head. "What's Willow planning to do with the ring?"

"She's got it on a chain round her neck," said Rick. "At first she said that we could both give it to mom for her birthday." He hesitated, "But I don't think she means it. She's really hooked on wearing it herself. She's always slipping it on her finger when she thinks no one's looking."

"It was a pretty neat thing to find," said Casey.

"Well, I've found something neat too," said Rick.

"Yeah, you told me about that picture you discovered in Ontario," said Casey.

"No, I'm talking about right here," said Rick. "But I'm not telling the family yet, either … specially Willow. Want to know what it is?"

Casey nodded.

"Promise not to tell."

"I promise."

Rick looked up and down the street to check no one was in earshot.

"It's a poem," he hissed.

Casey burst out laughing. "What do you mean, you 'found' a poem?" he sputtered.

"Shut up, you idiot … you'll give it away … I'm serious."

Rick dragged Casey to the riverbank and dropped his voice to a whisper again. "I really mean it. I think I've found a Robert Service poem, and you'll never guess where."

Casey shook his head, his eyes still twinkling.

"In the old cabin on your dad's claim."

Casey's eyes widened. "What! What do you mean?"

"It was hidden there," Rick said. "Squished up in the

insulation behind the wallboards." He explained how the paper had fallen out on top of him.

"So what did you do with it?" asked Casey.

"What do you think … it wasn't mine. I shoved it back … but I copied it out first." Rick pulled out his notebook and passed it over.

Casey read the poem. "Pretty cool," he said. "I've heard the story about the bishop who ate his boots — our teacher told us. But I've never heard of a poem based on it. How come you think Robert Service wrote it?"

"Well, I don't have any proof. There's no signature," admitted Rick. "But you've gotta admit it sounds like one of his."

Casey nodded.

"So I went on the Web and looked up a list of his poems. There isn't one about the bishop who ate his boots. So what if it's a new one? A poem that somehow missed being published? It sounds just like other stuff he wrote."

"It could be someone copying him," said Casey.

Rick nodded. "Yeah … but would they copy what he wrote with and what he wrote on? The words were written out in pencil on big sheets of paper, with stuff crossed out. That was how Robert Service wrote his poems. Jamie told us. The only thing is, how come they were stuffed in the wall at your cabin and weren't at the Robert Service cabin."

"I've got an idea. Let's go talk to Grandma," said Casey. "Her dad knew Robert Service."

"Really?" said Rick. "Okay. Where is she?"

"A few blocks away in the senior citizens' home. Come on.

She loves having visitors who want to know about the old days. You'll have to yell, though. She's real deaf and nearly blind."

Casey waved to the nurses and led the way to his grandma's room. She was sitting upright in a chair, peering closely at a piece of irregular multi-coloured knitting through thick glasses.

"That you, Casey?" she said. "Who's with you?"

"I'm Rick."

"Who?"

"Rick," bellowed Casey. "He's a friend. He wants to know about the old times. About Great-Grandad and Robert Service."

"The old times, is it." Grandma laughed. "Nothing but old times in this town. Sometimes think it went to sleep right after the gold rush."

Grandma peered around and rapped a small cupboard with her knitting needle. "Look in there. Might find some cookies. Boys like cookies, eh?" She peered up into Rick's face.

Rick grinned and nodded.

Casey pried the lid off the tin and held it out.

"Chocolate digestives ... great," said Rick.

"Take two — take two," said Grandma. "I never eat them. I just get them in for Casey. That way he comes to see me once in a while."

"Yeah, Grandma, I just come for the cookies," said Casey. "Tell us about the log cabin out at the claim, and Robert Service."

Grandma abandoned her knitting and laughed. "Oh, that old cabin. I used to play in it when I was a girl. Father was lucky. Struck it rich on his claim. He didn't have to live in the cabin out on the creek for long. He made his pile and built a house in town. Hired people to work for him."

"Did you know Robert Service?" Rick asked. "I've visited his cabin on Eighth Avenue."

Grandma tapped Rick's arm. "Speak up, young man."

"Robert Service," shouted Rick. "Did you know him?"

"Father knew him," said Grandma, "but I don't remember. I wasn't born when Mr. Service left Dawson. He was famous then." Grandma chuckled. "After he left town, the ladies used to hold teas up in his cabin on the edge of town and recite his poems." She shook her head. "He was a one, that man. So proper, always a banker. The stories Father told." She poked Rick with her knitting needles. "Want to know something?"

"Er, sure," said Rick.

"That man was so proper he couldn't survive in the real North on his own at first," said Grandma. "He just wrote about it. My father even let him stay in our old cabin on the claim, so he had a taste of living on the creeks."

Rick and Casey exchanged glances.

She laughed again. "Mr. Service hated it. Went out for a walk and got lost in the forest." She slapped her knee and chuckled. "Didn't know where he was without a road to follow! He only stayed for a week and couldn't get back into town fast enough."

"But he lived in a little log cabin in town," said Rick, puzzled.

"Ah, but it was easy in town, see," said Grandma. "Mr. Service didn't cook or anything. He'd go down to the hotel for his

96

meals and a girl would do his washing. All Mr. Service had to do was write his poems." Grandma shook her head. "He was a character. Real shy. Didn't mix much. Wrote all night long, then slept all morning. Father said he'd wander down to the hotel to eat breakfast in the middle of the afternoon."

Grandma gazed into the distance, remembering. "I saw some of his poems in his own writing once. When I was a child, Mother took me up to one of the ladies' teas on Eighth. Everyone laughed when I said the cabin was real untidy. He'd left bits of poetry pinned up on the wall, flapping around."

"What happened to them?" asked Rick.

Grandma looked at Rick through her glasses. "I think people took them for souvenirs — there's none left now."

"Did he write anything in your cabin on the creek?" asked Rick.

"Who knows," said Grandma. "It was a long time ago."

"So what do you think?" asked Rick as he and Casey jogged along the boardwalk toward the *Keno*.

Casey shrugged helplessly. "I guess it could be a Robert Service poem since he stayed in our cabin. But I still don't get why it would be stuffed in the wall!"

Rick thought for a moment. "What if … what if it was winter when he was out there?"

Casey nodded. "So?"

"Well, what if he didn't like what he'd written and was cold, so he screwed it up and stuffed it in the wall for more insulation."

Casey started to get excited. "What if he just left it hanging around and someone else used it as insulation?"

Rick nodded excitedly. "Yeah, that might have happened." Then his excitement faded. "But if the poem was written by Service, how come it wasn't published in one of his books?"

"Rick! Casey! Over here!" Willow jumped up and down, waving frantically.

The boys looked around. Willow was on the opposite corner.

"Over here, don't bother going to the *Keno*. We're in the Chinese restaurant," she called. "Mom sent me to find you."

The kids joined Marty and Shari in a booth.

"How was your morning?" asked Shari. "Where did you get to?"

"We visited Casey's grandma," said Rick. "Guess what. Her dad knew Robert Service."

Shari and Marty exchanged quick looks.

"Do you think she would mind if we interviewed her?" Shari asked Casey.

Casey burst out laughing. "Mind? She'd love it. It would make her day if she was in the movie."

Suddenly Rick slid down the booth and made himself inconspicuous.

"What's up with you?" asked Willow.

"Here comes trouble." Rick jerked his head toward the doorway.

Kate walked in, spotted them, and walked over. "Hi, all ready for the show?" she asked.

98

Rick nudged Willow and winked at Casey. He shook his head, looked miserable, and mouthing silent words, pointed to his throat.

"He's got a terrible sore throat," said Willow seriously.

"Lost his voice this morning," added Casey.

"What!" yelled Kate.

The three children dissolved in giggles.

"Ignore them," said Shari. "They're just winding you up. Rick will be in full voice for the concert tomorrow."

"Huh, I've already had the juggler cancel since the dress rehearsal," said Kate sourly. "He seemed to think a sprained wrist was an adequate excuse. I don't know what happened to the idea 'the show must go on!'" She fixed Rick and Willow with a steely gaze. "Don't forget to be at the theatre in good time. Bye." She went to sit at a table near the window.

Willow watched Kate surreptitiously. She couldn't make her out. Sometimes she was nice, sometimes she was less nice. She certainly seemed to pick on Rick. Willow's Web search was giving her conflicting messages. Then there was the strange business of the ring. Kate had never mentioned it since. But it was all too vague — it would be hard to discuss it with Mom without any hard information.

As Willow watched, Kate moved a used coffee cup and looked down at the table. Swiftly her hand shot out and disappeared into her pocket.

Willow's eyes widened. Had Kate just pinched a tip off the table?

CHAPTER NINE

There was no mistaking Discovery Days in Dawson. "Looks like the whole town's involved," said Willow, pointing excitedly to the parade winding onto Front Street, greeted by excited crowds on the boardwalks and people hanging out of upper-storey windows.

Bands were playing, balloons were flying (and occasionally popping), and the air was full of the smell of popcorn, hot dogs, and barbecued salmon from a massive grill set up by the river.

"I don't feel so bad about having to wear a costume this afternoon," said Rick suddenly. "Everyone is dressed up, even Casey." He jumped up and down waving madly as the float from the Tr'ondek Hwetch'in Cultural Centre trundled past.

Casey spotted them, grinned, and stuck out his leg to show off brand-new mukluks. "Grandma made them," he yelled. He hurled a handful of candy in Rick and Willow's direction.

Rick gave a thumbs-up.

The Forster-Jennings family wandered around enjoying the

activities. They cheered as people dressed as voyageurs canoed down the river and re-enacted the first landing of the Hudson's Bay traders. Rick and Willow tried gold panning in the Cheechako class but were beaten soundly by a six-year-old kid who had obviously been practising for weeks.

"That kid found his gold flakes in three minutes," complained Willow, as she tucked into a salmon burger. "I hadn't even got the first big rocks out by then." Still grumbling, she followed the rest of her family as they headed for the theatre.

It was chaos backstage, and Kate was running from side to side trying to answer three questions at once.

"I'm keeping out of her way," muttered Rick.

They edged through the crowd. Performers of all ages were grabbing costumes off racks and fighting for dressing room space. Dancers stretched, singers warmed up their voices, and musicians tuned and played snatches of melody.

Rick spotted bags labelled "Rick" and "Willow" containing their costumes and thrust Willow's into her arms. "Meet back here in five minutes," he said and disappeared into the men's dressing room.

Willow elbowed her way into the women's dressing room, claimed a corner of a mirror, and swiftly transformed herself into an 1890s belle. Bobbing a little curtsy to her reflection, she went to find Rick.

Rick stood rigidly at their meeting place. Beads of perspiration dotted his forehead and his face was white. "I can't do this." He grabbed Willow's arm. "I mean it. I can't go on stage. I — I — I'll throw up or something."

The Palace Grand Theatre

In Dawson's heyday, theatre troupes performed in tents and small wood frame buildings. Dawson's first theatre was a log-built "opera house," and several others were built before the Grand Opera House (later called the Palace Grand, The Savoy, and the Old Savoy) opened in 1899.

It was built by California-born entrepreneur and showman Arizona Charlie, who had been a cowboy, travelled to England with Buffalo Bill's Wild West Show, and toured his own show around the U.S. and Mexico. With a revolver, he shot cigarettes from his wife's mouth and glass balls from between her fingers. One night he shot her thumb off, and the act did not appear again.

The theatre showed drama, musical theatre, and vaudeville, after which the seats would be cleared for a dance. After years of heaving permafrost and rotting wood, the theatre became unsafe and was closed in 1940.

Parks Canada took over the old theatre in 1960. After careful study, it was replaced with a replica that was identical, right down to the wallpaper and light fixtures, and reopened in 1962. Parks Canada gives tours, and the theatre has a Klondike Follies show each summer for tourists and locals.

Willow stared at Rick, then dragged him through the throng of performers to a quiet corridor near the open fire escape door at the back of the theatre.

Rick sagged against the wall.

"Take some deep breaths," Willow whispered.

Rick nodded and concentrated on his breathing for a while. Gradually the colour came back to his cheeks. He grinned shakily at his sister. "Thanks. Don't know what got into me. I've done stuff like this before."

Willow grinned back. "It happened to me once. Don't forget, I threw up in Prince Charming's top hat."

Rick gave a shout of laughter.

"Quiet," yelled Kate from the end of the corridor, dropping her voice as she realized there was a sudden hush from the other side of the curtain. "We're about to start. Come along, come along."

They found a corner where they could stand and run over their lines but still hear their cue from the wings.

"Want me to hear you say 'The Spell of the Yukon'?" whispered Willow, after she had reread her poem a couple of times.

"No thanks," said Rick, surreptitiously stuffing sheets of handwritten paper back in his pocket. "I'll be okay when I get on stage."

Willow stared at his bulging pocket curiously. "Haven't you got it learned yet? I thought you were all right at dress rehearsal?"

Rick looked guilty and turned away quickly.

One of the dancers beckoned them over. She'd found a

place where one person at a time could peek at the audience without being seen.

Rick glued his eye to the gap and scanned the rows of people.

"Can you see Mom and Dad?" whispered Willow.

Rick shook his head. "They must be right at the back, filming. Casey's here, though, and his mom and dad." He moved away to let Willow peek.

"Jamie's here," she giggled. "He's still dressed as Robert Service. Do you think he has any other clothes?"

A poke in her back made her jump. Kate glared at them and waved them away. Rick and Willow flattened themselves against the wall as the curtain rose and an entire school band marched on stage for an uncertain "Oh Canada."

A brief speech by the mayor was followed by more band numbers, and the concert was launched.

Willow was nervous too. She waited through a series of acts, fingering her lucky nugget ring through her blouse.

Finally, a woman with a pink dress and a loud voice sang an old-fashioned ballad to a piano accompaniment full of twiddly bits, and Willow knew she was next.

"You're on," whispered Kate, her hand pushing firmly in the centre of Willow's back.

Willow slipped the nugget ring on and off her finger for luck and marched confidently to the centre of the stage. The lights dazzled her, and she could barely see the crowds in the auditorium. She gulped, then took a deep breath and announced in a clear voice, "The Cremation of Sam McGee, by Robert Service."

"There are strange things done in the midnight sun ..." she began, and immediately felt the audience settle back to enjoy the familiar words.

After a couple of verses, she was openly enjoying herself with the bizarre story of the gold miner who was never warm in the Yukon until he died, and his friend cremated him in the boiler of an old steamboat.

Willow's voice rang round the hall in the final verse as she described how the furnace doors were flung open, and there was Sam sitting in the middle of the flames saying, *"Since I left Plumtree, down in Tennessee, it's the first time I've been warm."*

She marched off stage to laughter, applause, and several cheers.

Rick slapped her back. "Way to go, Willow," he said. "But be sure not to miss mine."

"Course not," said Willow, puzzled. She squeezed his arm. "You'll be fine."

Rick waited nervously by the curtains. A pair of teenage ballet dancers twirled around in tutus, then the lady with the pink dress was back for another song. At last, his turn came, and Rick too felt Kate's firm hand in the small of his back.

I'll fix her, he thought, as he marched on stage.

Rick looked at the rows of faces — and froze. His knees trembled, his mind went blank and his throat dry. The audience silently stared up at him.

"The Spell of the Yukon," hissed Kate from the wings.

That was all he needed. "In your dreams," thought Rick. He shot a triumphant look at Kate, took a deep breath, and hitched his thumbs in his suspenders.

"The Bishop Who Ate His Boots," Rick announced, then paused. "By Robert Service — I think," he added.

A buzz of interest ran through the audience.

Kate clapped her hand to her forehead and took a step forward with arms outstretched as if she were going to drag Rick off stage.

Casey giggled, stuffed a handkerchief in his mouth, and fell off his chair.

Rick ignored them all, and began.

There's many a tale told on the trail, by men who grub for gold,
'Neath northern lights, on freezing nights, they huddle in cabins cold.
They scoff their sourdough bread with beans, then each rolls in his bed,
And takes his turn to call to mind a feast on which he's fed.

Mike spun a tale of London town, of caviar in the Strand,
While Joe remembered Christmas goose, the fattest in the land,
"But there's none enjoyed their food," said Sam, "like the bishop who bared his feet,
And boiled his boots for seven hours, then served them up to eat."

The bishop's way was long that day, o'er mountain, hill and
vale,
Then snow swept in, a blizzard's din, and he lost sight of the
trail,
He sat on his sack with rock at his back, and fire to keep him
warm.
He brewed his tea and hugged his knee, and waited out the
storm.

The blizzard's bite he felt all night, and it ranted through next
day,
He peered around his rock but found he could not see the way.
He stirred his fire till flames rose higher, and sipped his
dwindling store.
"Good Lord," he said, "if you don't want me dead, I'll need a
wee bit more."

He heaped the fire while drifts piled higher, and walled the
bishop in.
He dreamed of dishes heaped with fishes, and loaves that
steamed in the tin.
He groaned with hunger in despair, and stamped his freezing
foot.
"The end is nigh," he seemed to sigh, then his eye lit on his
boot.

"The skin of a seal might make a meal, for a man in such a
spot."

He boiled his boots for seven hours and supped them piping
  hot.
To the starving man his cooking pan put forth a smell
  incredible,
"Fillet of sole," the Bishop said, "I used to think inedible."

The bishop chewed his footwear stewed, and said, "It's rather
  tough."
Each morsel downed, the bishop frowned, "That's fine. But not
  enough."
Then Bishop Stringer with his finger finished off the stew,
"Thanks, Lord," he said. "I'm still not dead. Let's see how the
  laces chew."

Rick bowed.

There was a pause, then the whole audience was on its feet clapping, stamping, hooting, and hollering.

"Where did you get that, kid?" someone shouted.

"Nice poem!" called out Jamie's voice.

Rick stood in astonishment. "Holy cow," he muttered. He looked into the wings. Kate, hand on hip, frowned and beckoned to him. Rick turned and looked at the other side of the stage. Willow waved, and he ran and joined her.

"What did you do, little brother?" she laughed, grabbing his arm. "Let's go and find Mom." They sneaked round to the back of the hall as the church choir filed on stage.

They slumped into the seats Shari had saved for them. "Was that what you were supposed to recite?" she whispered.

 Isaac Stringer, the bishop who really did eat his boots, was born in Ontario in 1866. He decided to become a missionary in the Canadian North. He learned something about medicine and practised pulling teeth on his father. By the summer of 1892 he was in Fort McPherson, down the Mackenzie River.

Stringer learned Inuktitut, the Inuit language. In 1893, he travelled to remote Herschel Island, in the Arctic Ocean, was ordained as an Anglican minister, and worked to improve the way whalers dealt with the natives. Stringer started schools, provided medicine, and raised a family in the Mackenzie Delta. In 1905, he became bishop in Yukon Territory and moved to Dawson.

In 1909, he took a long journey through his old territory, and in September headed out through the mountains to return to Dawson. Difficult travel conditions, and shortage of help and game, left the bishop and one companion stranded in the wild without food in late October. For four days they had only the bishop's boots to eat, but then they found help at a First Nations fishing camp and managed to complete their journey.

In 1931, Stringer became Archbishop of Rupert's Land and died in Winnipeg in 1934, still in office.

www.dawsoncity.org/stories_Bishop_Eats_Boots.htm

Rick shook his head.

"What do you think you were playing at?" growled Kate, coming up behind them.

Jamie appeared on Rick's other side. "Where did that little wonder come from?" he whispered.

The choir launched into their number.

"Shhhh." People sitting nearby turned to glare.

Rick slunk down on the nearest chair and tried to disappear in the dark.

Once the show was over, Rick couldn't hide any more. He found himself backed into a corner surrounded by Kate, Jamie, and a bunch of Robert Service fans.

"But where did the poem come from?" said Jamie. "The story's familiar, and it sounds like Service, but I've never even heard of it."

"I found it. In an old cabin," Rick explained. "I copied it out. It was written on big sheets of paper shoved in the wall."

There was a gasp from several people in the crowd.

"That I need to see," said Jamie, his eyes lighting up. "If it really is a Robert Service poem, and it's in his own handwriting — do you know how rare and valuable that would be?"

Kate stiffened. Her eyes widened. She moved closer to Rick and Jamie.

Rick looked startled. "I kinda thought people might be interested in the poem, but I didn't know it was worth money." He stood on tiptoe and searched the crowd for Casey and his parents.

"We'd need to collect the paper carefully and have it

110

examined and the handwriting verified," said Jamie. "Do you know whose cabin it is?"

Rick nodded.

"Could we get permission to go there?" said Jamie eagerly. Kate leaned forward.

Rick looked uncomfortable. "Dunno. I'll ask C... ouch!"

Willow, watching Kate's face, had stomped on Rick's foot. "If it's valuable, I don't think you should say anything more," she said sensibly. "There are too many people around."

Kate flushed and eased back a little.

Jamie looked up, surprised at the size of the crowd that had gathered behind him. He patted Rick's shoulder. "Sorry, I got carried away with enthusiasm. Willow's right." He sighed. "Look, all the Parks staff are tied up with Discovery Days this weekend, but I'd be really interested in talking to the owner of the cabin as soon as it's over. Will you explain what's happened and ask if we can contact them next week?"

"Sure," said Rick.

The crowd dispersed, still talking and arguing about the new poem and if it really was by Robert Service.

"Well, son." Marty appeared and mussed Rick's hair. "You certainly caused a stir." He patted the camera. "And we've caught it all on tape." He headed for the door, shouldering his camera.

Rick ducked under his arm. "Back in a minute. I've gotta find Casey and his dad.

Kate's eyes widened. She pushed through the crowd after Rick.

Willow watched, frowning, then slipped quietly after her.

CHAPTER TEN

Willow tossed and turned uneasily in her bunk. She thought about the poem Rick had found and, in her mind, put together a jigsaw of bits and pieces she had observed. Finally, she could lie there no longer. Even though Casey was sleeping over in Rick's room and she'd promised not to bug them, she had to talk! She swung her legs off the bunk and tiptoed to Rick's door.

Willow knocked quietly. "Rick, Casey, can I come in? You're not asleep yet, are you?" Rick grunted.

She opened the door and slipped inside the tiny bedroom. Shar Cho stood up and wagged his tail in greeting. She patted his head absently. It was grey and gloomy, for Rick had pulled down his blind against the midnight sun. She stepped carefully over Casey, curled up in a sleeping bag on the floor, then hitched up onto Rick's bed and perched cross-legged by his feet. "I've been thinking!" she hissed.

Rick groaned and sat up. His hair stuck out over his head. "We're asleep. What's up? What time is it?"

"Midnight, but I need to talk to you, so keep your voice

113

down. With the cast party, and Mom and Dad chasing us straight to bed, we've never had a moment alone since the show," Willow whispered.

Rick grinned. "Good, wasn't it?" he whispered back.

Willow chuckled quietly. "You sure stirred things up. Anyway … I need to talk to you about the cabin, and Kate."

"I got her good, didn't I," said Rick with satisfaction. "I'm just sorry I couldn't see her face."

"I could," said Willow. "It was great. She nearly dragged you off stage a couple of times. But listen, you're right. She's trouble."

Rick peered at Willow through the dim light. "You've changed your tune."

"I've done some more digging on the Net," said Willow. "I tried before but couldn't find much when I just typed in 'Kate' as her first name. But then I realized that Kate is probably just a short version of her real name. Mom said if she was Dutch her name might be Katerina. So while I was doing the laundry, I tried again. I found an archived newspaper story about a Katerina Van Sacker who was in some trouble at a museum in Ontario while she was a volunteer there. She'd told me she volunteered at a museum, but of course I can't prove it was her, so I haven't said anything to anybody. Then there was the strange business with the Klondike ring. And I'm sure I saw her pinch a tip off the table in the Chinese restaurant."

Rick gave a snort of disgust.

"You should have seen Kate's face when Jamie said the

114

poem could be worth money. She stiffened. It was like her ears pricked up," continued Willow.

Rick rolled over and switched on his bedroom light. "What?" he said, rubbing his eyes with his fists and hauling himself up on one elbow.

Casey sat up. He blinked a couple of times and stared sleepily at Willow and Rick.

"And after I trod on your foot to shut you up, she followed you," finished Willow. "She was spying on you, Rick! She watched you talking and laughing with Casey's dad, and I think she guessed the poem was found in his cabin. I saw her face. She suddenly looked really triumphant."

"You mean …" Rick struggled to put everything together. "If Kate knows where the poem is, she could go and get it?"

"Exactly," said Willow.

Casey yawned. "What's the big deal? The Parks staff are going to collect it, and she's with Parks."

"She's not going to give it to Parks," said Willow positively. "She'll sell it for money."

"We can't prove that," said Rick, yawning again.

"No," said Willow. "But we can't risk it either."

"Then we'd better get the poem first," said Rick. "In the morning, before the raft race. Goodnight."

He turned over and closed his eyes, and Willow slipped out of the room.

After breakfast, Rick and Willow had got the okay to hang out with Casey before the race. "We're filming the raft race,"

Marty had pointed out. "Don't you want to come down with us and see it?"

"It's okay, Dad," Rick told him. "We're going up to the claim. We'll get a ride down with Casey and see you there."

With Casey and Shar Cho, they walked up the trail toward the cabin.

"Shh," said Rick. "There's a truck parked near the road. It's probably nothing to do with us, but — "

Shar Cho gave a growl deep in his throat. Casey's hand shot out and touched his muzzle. "Quiet boy," he whispered. Shar Cho obeyed.

They advanced closer. Casey pointed to the alder thicket and everyone nodded. They lay down in the shadows and watched. The cabin looked peaceful, and the door was open as it had been when Rick and Willow first saw it.

"Did you leave the door open?" whispered Casey.

Rick shook his head. "I shut it so the bear wouldn't get inside."

They listened. Rustling sounds came from inside the cabin.

Rick went white. "The bear's back!"

Casey shook his head. "Those aren't bear noises." He began to wriggle forward on his stomach through the undergrowth. Willow and Rick followed. They wriggled right to the edge of the veranda and slowly raised their heads to look inside.

The cabin was not empty. A figure in khaki shirt and pants was pulling piece after piece of paper out from behind the wallboard. Several pieces were already smoothed and spread out on the floor.

CRACK! Willow knelt on a twig.

The figure swung around. It was Kate!

Rick and Casey ran up the steps.

"You're trespassing," said Casey.

"Leave that alone. It's not yours," Rick said.

Kate's jaw dropped. The hand holding a sheet of paper shook. She took a breath and bared her teeth in a fixed smile.

"Parks decided to take charge of the poem immediately," she said. Her voice had none of its usual authority. "Fragile heritage property shouldn't stay in an old cabin where it can be damaged." She placed the sheet on the pile.

"So why sneak up here early, on a day when everybody's busy with the raft race?" asked Willow. "In fact, how come you're not busy with the raft race? You're organizing it."

Kate flushed but spread her hands and eyes wide. "P — Parks told me to come here."

Casey shook his head. "That's not true. My dad's arranged to bring Jamie and some other Parks people here next week."

"You're taking the poem for yourself, aren't you?" accused Willow.

Kate's eyes flashed. "You'd better think twice before you make accusations like that," she growled. "There, that's the lot." She rolled the papers neatly, inserted them into a plastic tube, snapped on the ends, and walked out the door. "Run away and play," she added rudely. She strode quickly down the riverbank, the roll in her hand.

"She's stealing the poem," said Rick.

"We'll fix that," said Casey. "Rick, you follow her. We'll run for the raft."

"The raft?" said Willow. "How's that going to help?"

"Trust me," said Casey.

The three friends ran to the riverbank. Rick followed Kate down the bank, Casey grabbed life jackets he had cached under a bush, and Willow untied the rope.

Casey leaped on as it bobbed in the current. "Give her a push," he yelled.

Casey and Willow leaned on their poles and eased the raft into faster water. Shar Cho whined from the bank, unsure what to do, then padded along the bank beside them.

As they passed Rick, he leaped aboard.

Casey handed his pole to Rick. "Keep her going. And watch this."

The stream narrowed and the current picked up. As the raft drifted up to her, Kate looked around at the sound of their voices. She did not speak but was obviously angry that they were following her.

Casey whistled a piercing note through his teeth. Shar Cho's ears pricked up. The dog looked eagerly toward Casey and cocked his head.

Casey pointed after Kate. "Stick, Shar Cho. Fetch the stick."

Shar Cho ran after Kate. He jumped, snatching the plastic tube from her hand.

"Hey," yelled Kate. "Drop it!" She gave chase.

Shar Cho ran swiftly along the bank, Kate pounding behind him.

"Good dog," called Casey. "Now come." He slapped the raft. Shar Cho splashed into the water. To yells of encouragement from the kids, he swam, holding the roll in his jaws high above the water.

"Good dog," said Casey, as he leaned over the raft and grabbed the ruff on Shar Cho's neck. He and Rick hauled the sodden dog up onto the logs. The raft tipped sharply and then stabilized.

"Give," Casey ordered.

Shar Cho dropped the roll into his hand, and Willow cheered.

The kids looked back at Kate, as she stopped, out of breath, and shook her fist.

Suddenly the raft gave a little shudder and swirled around as one corner bounced off a rock.

"Hey, I can't hold it!" yelled Willow. "Get your poles in and help get us across the stream. The current's got us."

It was no use. Even with all three pushing on their poles, they were being swept into the centre of the stream and round a corner.

The raft swept under the plank bridge that led to Pete's claim, and Kate was out of sight. The banks were now heavily wooded, and there was no place to land. After a vigorous shake which showered them all, Shar Cho lay quietly in the middle of the logs, one paw protectively over his "stick" as the kids struggled to keep the raft stable in the fast current. Under Casey's instructions they managed to avoid rocks and shallows and took turns poling so they could put on their life jackets. They were just beginning to feel they could manage the raft when it rounded another corner and they found themselves out in the main channel of the Klondike River. As they emerged, a shot from a starting pistol rang out.

Casey began to laugh. "Oops, we've done it now!" he said as their raft joined a row of other rafts carrying costumed figures. "We've joined the raft race."

"Oh, no. We're in big trouble," groaned Willow.

Casey and Rick exchanged glances.

"Not if we win," said Rick. His mouth set firmly as he thrust his pole into the river and the raft shot forward.

"Come on, crew." Casey fended them off a passing gravel bank. "We wanted to do this. Now's our chance. Get poling!"

The Klondike was swift, wide, and shallow, and the raft was buffeted through small rapids and waves. Casey manned the front and Rick and Willow each manned a side. Shar Cho sat in the middle in a regal pose, gazing around with interest. They were already in the main current — the difficulty was to stay there with all the other rafts jostling for the best spots.

Rick clutched his pole firmly and watched what was happening to the other rafts. One drifted into shallow water and went aground, its crew yelling and bouncing up and down trying to jiggle the raft free. Another raft floated under a high bank and became caught up in fallen trees that leaned over into the water.

"We've got to keep in the middle!" Rick shouted.

Casey nodded. "Concentrate on the water. Watch for the ripples and waves that mean submerged rocks. Steer around them."

The river took a wide sweep and passed an RV park, where two elderly couples waved as the rafts bobbed past.

One raft carrying a crew dressed as gold rush miners and their girls swept ahead to hoots and hollers, then another raft swirled close to them, barely missing a collision.

"Good grief. What the heck are you kids doing?" called a familiar voice. Jamie and his crew, all four dressed as Robert Service, laughed and waved. "Sorry guys, I guess we're ahead."

"Don't count your chickens," Casey shouted, easing the raft again into the strongest current.

"There's a bridge coming up fast," warned Willow.

She had no sooner spoken than the miners' raft hit the bank and capsized. A man with a movie camera leaned over the bridge rail to catch the action.

"Oh no," Willow groaned. "Dad's filming us."

Rick bent his head down and pulled his cap over his eyes.

Casey didn't care. "Hi, Mr. Forster," he yelled as their raft swept under the bridge.

Rick and Willow gripped their poles tighter as they swirled under the bridge. At first it had been exciting, but now they were getting tired. The water kept changing. Smooth fast reaches were followed by choppy water full of rocks, and the main channel snaked between rocks and sandbanks, first in the middle of the stream and then running close to the banks.

They were now way ahead of most of the flotilla, and only the Robert Service raft was ahead of them.

Then the broad waters of the Yukon River came in sight in the distance. On the right, the dike at the edge of town was lined with people.

"Jamie's raft is going to win," said Willow. She pointed to a couple of powerboats anchored on each side of the river, with the finishing rope stretched between them.

"What a run though," said Rick enthusiastically. "Let's give it our best finish."

Willow suddenly realized they were passing the spot where she'd found the Klondike ring. She ran her fingers down the chain around her neck and clutched the ring tight. Closing her eyes, she made a gigantic wish.

"Watch out," yelled Casey. "Man overboard!"

Jamie's raft had hit a submerged boulder, and the jolt sent one of the Robert Services into the water with a great splash. Shar Cho leaped to his feet and howled.

There was much laughter and applause from the watchers on the dike as the crew struggled to pull their shipmate back on board and to free the raft.

"Hey, this is our chance!" yelled Rick. The three children bent and poled and pushed and shoved to force their raft to sweep past the leader.

Frantic yells erupted behind them. Two other rafts had collided with Jamie's raft. One promptly disintegrated and the logs swept downstream. The crew members splashed through the waist-high water to the shore, to be greeted

The Discovery Days raft race was an echo of the great armada of boats and rafts that brought the Klondikers to Dawson in 1898. Thousands of would-be miners had made their way over the Chilkoot and White Passes from Alaska. Mounties met them at the summits and insisted that they have a year's supplies or they would be turned back. The Klondikers camped around Lake Bennett, cut down trees, and built a motley collection of rafts and boats. Some were experienced; others had no idea how to build and navigate a vessel.

On May 29, the ice began to break up, and 7124 vessels set sail. Some were paddled or rowed, others wind propelled as tents were turned into sails. It was a race! The first to get to Dawson, everyone thought, had the best chance of gold nuggets.

The Yukon River was generally broad and swift, but there were lakes where wind can upset boats, and severe rapids near Whitehorse and at other places along the way. Some Klondikers drowned; others lost their outfits when boats capsized. No one knows how many boats made it to Dawson, but the population rose to almost 40,000 people.

www.yukonlearn.com/pub/klondike/page23.htm
www.yukonlearn.com/pub/klondike/page25.htm

with more laughter and cheers. But the collision freed Jamie's raft.

"Don't look back," commanded Captain Casey. "Concentrate on the rope. We're nearly there." He strained to keep the raft in the strongest flow, and they swept under the rope to a cry of "The winners!" from both boats and the crowd on the bank. Willow reached for her ring again, and whispered, "Thank you."

Jamie's crew sailed under the rope a few metres behind them.

A grinning First Nations fisherman in a powerboat tossed a tow rope to Casey.

"Hi, Uncle Mark," said Casey. "Thanks."

"Couldn't bear to stay on dry land, eh Casey?" Mark smiled. "Anybody would think you were one of the river people!" He took up the slack and towed them toward shore.

"Wow," said Rick. "That was fun."

"Yeah, wicked," said Casey.

"Only now we're all in trouble," said Willow. She had spied Casey's dad and her mother waiting together on the beach.

"We couldn't help it," said Rick, following her eyes and practising his best pleading tone.

"No," said Willow. "But who's going to believe us? And what's Kate going to say when she gets here?"

CHAPTER ELEVEN

Pete and Shari met in the centre of the cheering crowd as the first raft was being towed in.

"Came in first," said Pete proudly. "That's my boy."

"But they shouldn't have been in the race," said Shari. "We didn't know."

"Hey, I didn't know either. But Casey knows the river. He's built a lot of rafts, and he knows to wear safety gear."

"I guess that's something," said Shari. "But they should have asked."

Many willing hands held the raft steady while Casey, Willow, and Rick stepped onto the beach to earsplitting whoops and cheers. They were closely followed by Shar Cho clutching the plastic cylinder in his mouth. Suddenly everyone was talking at once.

Casey's school friends gathered round with high fives, while adults patted their backs, and tourists snapped their pictures and muttered into the microphones of their video cameras.

"Attaboy," said Pete, clapping Casey on the shoulder. "They came in first," he added to the crowd at large.

"Do you know how dangerous rafting down the river could have been?" said Shari, fixing Rick and Willow with a steely gaze.

"You can't win. Your raft's disqualified," said the chief judge to Casey. "You're all under age."

"Hey, give the kids a break," called a voice in the crowd. "They ran a great race."

"Yeah. They're the winners all right."

People around them cheered again.

"It was an accident, Mom," explained Rick. "We didn't mean to join the race."

"It wasn't dangerous, honestly," added Casey. "I build rafts all the time. I taught Willow and Rick how to pole and we had life jackets."

Shari nodded. "But we didn't know where you were."

"I said we'd get a ride with Casey and see you at the raft race," said Rick innocently. "Here we are."

Shari laughed and hugged them both. "And I'm glad you're safe, but we need to talk about this. Why don't we go up to the bus."

"We'd better go too," said Pete Eriksen. "Make way for the winners."

"But they didn't win," said the judge again. "They're disqualified."

"Garbage," said voices in the crowd. "Good for the kids, I say."

126

"Yeah, the youngsters won fair and square."

There were more cheers as Jamie and the Robert Service crew staggered up the beach.

The judge clapped Jamie on the back. "Congratulations! Your raft is the winner."

"Heck, no," said Jamie. "The kids beat us to it. They did the whole course. We nearly beat them, but they steered better than we did."

There was a round of applause at his remarks. The judges got in a huddle.

Rick nudged Casey, "What about the poem?"

Casey slapped his forehead and turned to Shar Cho. "Give!"

Shar Cho obediently dropped the plastic roll into Rick's outstretched hand.

"Here," Rick thrust the tube toward Casey's dad. "You'd better have this. It's the sheets of paper with the Robert Service poem."

Pete Eriksen stared. "Pardon?"

"The sheets from your cabin," explained Rick.

"What?" yelped Jamie. "What on earth were you kids thinking of? How could you? It was really important that we saw the sheets in situ and photographed and collected them carefully. Do you know how delicate old paper is?" He stared in horror at the water-splashed plastic tube. "Goodness knows what damage you've done."

Willow flushed. "Don't yell. We didn't do it. We rescued the poem. It was Kate Van Sacker that stole it."

127

"Yeah," said Casey. "We got it back for you." He looked up at his father. "Honestly, Dad."

"Kate!" said Jamie. "Kate works for Parks. Why would she steal it?"

"Well, she did," Willow insisted. "What else was she doing at the cabin early this morning? We saw her. She was taking the papers out of the wall and packing them in this tube. Did you ask her to do that?"

Jamie looked puzzled and shook his head. "No. We were going to the cabin with Mr. Eriksen on Tuesday."

"See!" said Casey triumphantly.

Jamie looked thunderstruck. "I'd better talk to Kate," he said and strode off.

Shari looked at her children. "I need to know more about this. Go on, back to the bus. We need to sort this out in private." Rick and Willow stomped up the bank.

Shari turned to Pete. "Would you and Casey like to come too?"

"Okay," said Pete. "And I don't like people taking things from my claim without permission, so I'll decide what happens to the poem from now on." He tucked the tube under his arm and strode up the bank after Shari. "Come on, Casey," he called over his shoulder.

Casey rolled his eyes and followed.

The judges came out of their huddle to discover that none of the riders of the first and second rafts were in sight. The chief judge threw up his hands. "What sort of event is this?"

"Chaotic?" called a voice from the crowd.

In the bus, Pete and Shari looked at the children. "You know you're supposed to tell us where you go and what you do," said Shari.

"But it wasn't our fault," said Willow promptly.

Her mother's face darkened.

"No, really Mom, Mr. Eriksen," said Rick. "It *wasn't* our fault we were in the raft race. The raft got away on us."

"We'd just made the raft to fool around on the creek," added Casey.

"And we got caught in the current when we stopped Kate from taking the poem," explained Willow.

Shari put a hand up to her forehead. "I still don't understand any of this, and I really don't have time. Your dad and I are in the middle of the shoot. I had to leave him to come and get you. Have you any idea how we felt when we saw you going under the bridge on that raft?"

Rick grinned unrepentantly, then caught his mother's eye and tried to look sorry. It didn't work.

"You'd better stay with us until we've finished filming," said Shari. "I've got to go back to help Marty. Our jobs are on the line."

"You know," said Pete, "it's all plausible. I know Casey makes rafts up the creek, and I don't mind. And if Kate was in my cabin stealing things, I'm really happy that your kids dealt with her. And if they escaped from Kate on the raft, the stream does run out into the Klondike. I know we don't have time to hear the whole story now, but you want to keep these kids out of more trouble. I've got a suggestion," said Pete.

"Could they go with Casey?" He held up his hand as she was about to interrupt. "—I know someone who'd love their company. All three of them can spend the afternoon visiting Grandma!"

Casey's grandma was bright-eyed and sparkly. She loved visitors. She sat up proudly. Here were her grandson, and his friends Willow and Rick, sitting in the residents' lounge entertaining everyone with the story of the poem Rick had discovered and how he'd recited it at the concert.

"Wish I could have been there," said her friend Emily. "Tell us how it went, lad."

"Yes. Go on, Rick. Give us a recitation. Speak up," encouraged Grandma. She leaned forward with her hand cupped around her ear.

Rick launched into "The Bishop Who Ate His Boots."

The old people cackled.

Emily nodded and wiped her streaming eyes. "Well done, lad, well done."

"I remember that story," said Grandma slowly. Her eyes seemed to gaze into the past. "Dad told me that Sadie Stringer, the bishop's wife, used to tell that tale over and over, every time she met a visitor from outside." Grandma shook her head. "But I never heard the poem before."

"I think it's a lost Robert Service poem," said Rick. "That's why I was asking you about him last time we came." He and Casey explained where it had been found — insulating the walls of the old cabin.

"That old place," said Grandma. "I hated staying there. It was always cold. Now what's all this about a raft?"

"How did you hear about that?" asked Casey. "Sure, we built a raft."

"Yeah, we got ways of hearing news without your wide world whatsit and your cellphones. I heard about it," said Grandma. "Heard you came in first."

"But we weren't entered in the race," said Willow.

"We weren't even allowed to enter the race," said Rick. So they told that story as well.

"You kids," laughed Grandma. "Always up to tricks. Well, I was pretty much the same. I got up to things I shouldn't." Her eyes took on a faraway look. "There used to be a bridge across the Klondike when I was a little girl. It went from Dawson to Klondike City — Lousetown we called it."

"Near where the raft race finished?" asked Willow.

Grandma nodded. "Mama would never let me cross — said the women who lived over in Lousetown weren't nice to know. They earned their money dancing with miners. Well, I didn't see anything wrong with that — Papa was a miner, and Mama danced with him. I was curious, wanted to go see. One day — I must have been eight," she said. "The bridge was empty, so I figured I could get over without anyone seeing me and telling my folks. I wanted to take a look around Lousetown and see what was so wicked about it."

"Did you get caught?" asked Willow.

"No, it was a quiet afternoon," said Grandma. "I was disappointed. It was just like Dawson, only the houses were

131

closer together and the streets narrower. There were cabins and stores, all kinds of stuff. I wandered where I liked and no one took no notice of me. Then I heard a dog barking, and a child crying. I went to see what was happening. There was this girl younger than me cowering against a wall, terrified of the dog barking at her. She thought it was going to bite her. The dog was a big mutt like our dog at home so I yelled at it and picked up a stick, and it slunk off. I asked the little girl to show me where she lived, and I carried her home.

"She lived in a poky cabin down a muddy alley, and her mama was at the door looking up and down for her. Her mama was beautiful. She wore a lovely blue silk dress with lace at the neck and wrists and lots of gold nugget jewellery. She dressed much fancier than my mama. She was real pleased with me for bringing her little girl home and took me in and gave me tea, and a piece of cake — delicious cake with white frosting.

"When I said I had to go, she pulled off a gold ring from her pinkie and gave it to me as a thank-you present. It had a big gold nugget in the middle and I'd never been given anything so beautiful. I put it on one of my fingers, gave her a hug and ran back across the bridge.

"Halfway across, a terrible thought struck me — there was no way I could take that ring home. If my mama knew I had crossed the bridge to Lousetown, I'd be in real trouble." Grandma smiled at the children. "In those days we were scared of our parents. We got lickin's."

The boys grinned.

"How could I tell my mama why I'd been given a valuable nugget ring? And I had nowhere to hide it. I shared a bedroom with my three sisters and there was no privacy, no secret hiding places."

While Grandma was talking, Willow fingered the Klondike ring through her shirt. Her face grew pale.

"I was young and didn't realize how valuable the ring was," continued Grandma. "I just knew it wasn't worth a lickin'. So I took it off my finger — and I threw it into the river."

Rick and Casey stared at each other, then both looked at Willow.

"I've often thought about that ring," said Grandma. "I didn't get many presents as a child. It was so special to have a gift like that."

Willow slowly pulled the chain out of her shirt and detached the ring.

She held it out to Casey's grandma. "Could this be your ring? We found it in the river gravel where the old bridge used to be."

Grandma squinted at the ring and held it in the light. Her eyes filled with tears. "Oh my ... oh my! It's just like my ring. Where did you find it again?"

Willow told the story of her find while Grandma looked at the ring in her palm. Then she tried to put it on her middle finger, but it was too tight. Then she laughed through her tears. "I wore it on that finger," she said, "but I guess I've grown a bit since then. Of course it won't fit there now." She slid it onto her little finger, then she reached out for Willow's hand and clutched it.

"Thank you, thank you, Willow. I never thought I'd see this again." Grandma sat looking at her ring, tears pouring down her cheeks.

Casey kissed her, and he, Rick, and Willow crept away leaving Grandma with her memories.

Later that afternoon Rick and Willow told the whole story to Marty and Shari. Their parents had accepted that the raft race caper was an accident and were glad that no one had got hurt. After more explanations, Marty and Shari also understood why the kids hadn't felt they had enough evidence to discuss Kate with them earlier. In fact, they were still concerned that Rick and Willow might have made a mistake somewhere along the way.

Marty pointed out how hard it was to prove that a poem was by a particular person, since people wrote imitations and made forgeries. Shari explained that many people had the same names, and the computer information Willow had found about Kate might refer to someone else, or indeed several people. Marty pointed out that Kate might have genuinely lost a ring, no matter how oddly she dealt with it. And Willow couldn't be sure Kate had stolen a tip in the restaurant — and even if she had, pocketing a couple of dollars was a long way from theft of an important heritage property. Maybe she just needed change and had added the amount to her own tip. And how could they be sure, Shari had asked, that Kate wasn't doing what she was doing in the cabin at the request of Parks, even if she had neglected to talk to the landowner first. You might well be right, was their parents' verdict, but it would be awful hard to prove if Kate were to deny everything.

Now Rick was reading, while Willow, worn out by the emotion of the afternoon, was asleep. Rick heard knocking on the bus door followed by the hum of voices. But he didn't stir — he was in a huff. Their parents hadn't really believed them and he was still mad.

Raps came on their bedroom doors. "Willow, Rick, I've got something to tell you," called Shari.

Neither Rick nor Willow answered.

Running footsteps pounded up the corridor and a fist hammered on each bedroom door. "Get your butts out of there. You'll never guess what's happened," shouted Casey. "It's Kate. She's done a bunk!"

"It's true," said Jamie, as Casey, Willow, and Rick erupted into the living area. "Kate cleared out her room and left town while we were all at the raft race. And she's taken a Parks vehicle without permission."

Casey's dad grinned. "You'll catch her. She must have gone south. There's really only one road out of town."

Jamie grinned back at him. "Yup. I've alerted the RCMP about the stolen truck, and she'll be picked up in Whitehorse."

He looked at the children. "I think we'd all better sit

down and listen to why you think she was stealing the poem."

Jamie was interrupted by another rap on the glass of the bus door.

There stood the chief judge from the raft race. "It took me a while to track you folks down," he grumbled. "No entry form meant no address. I've had to check three different campgrounds." He thrust small glass vials into each of the children's hands. "Popular opinion prevailed," he said in a surly tone. "It shouldn't have, but it did. You weren't awarded the first prize." He pointed at Jamie. "His raft was declared the winner even though he wasn't there to receive the cup and the gold bar."

The judge turned back to the children. "I've been instructed to give you special consolation prizes for the race. Good day." He stomped off as they chorused their thanks.

Willow, Rick, and Casey examined their vials. In each was a small gold nugget.

"Kate was short of money," said Willow after the excitement had died down. "She liked expensive clothes and stuff but was always complaining about being really broke and desperate to pay off her student loans. She did a whole bunch of stupid things to get money."

Willow told the whole story from the first meeting with Kate on the bus to the finding of the Klondike ring, Kate's phone calls about the ring, the stealing of the tip, and Kate spying on Rick and Mr. Eriksen. "But as Mom and Dad said, there was nothing certain we could tell anyone about," she finished. "It could all have had some other explanation. Even her taking the poem could have been because someone from Parks asked her to." She shrugged. Everyone looked at Jamie.

"She hadn't been in her office today," said Jamie, "and nobody knew where she was. I've talked to her boss, and certainly nobody in Parks had asked her to get the poem. And while I was in his office, the regional office rang and said they hadn't been able to verify all her qualifications and could she send more details. I'm wondering if maybe she didn't have the qualifications she used to get the job. So I went to the place she was staying. Her landlady says Kate told her her credit cards are being rejected and she owes money to almost every store in town. And the landlady heard she lost a whack at Diamond Gertie's gambling saloon the other night. That young lady certainly is broke."

"Well, I'll be blowed," said Pete Eriksen. "It's like something on TV."

It was evening. The Forster-Jennings family and the Eriksens had joined forces for an impromptu barbecue beside the river. Now the adults were talking over coffee, and the children were skipping stones across the water.

"Grandma's thrilled about the ring," said Casey. "She's told the story to half the town."

Willow smiled sadly. "I suppose deep down I always knew it wasn't really mine. It was beautiful, though."

what are we going to give to Mom for her birth-
[...] Rick. "It's tomorrow and we don't have anything
else."

"We'll buy something tomorrow morning," said Willow.
"But we don't have enough money for those nugget earrings
unless Dad'll help us."

"You want nugget earrings?" said Casey. "You've just been
given two gold nuggets."

"So?" said Rick.

"Give them to my mom. She'll make them into earrings
for you. It only takes her a few minutes to solder them onto
the mounts. I bet she'd do it tomorrow morning."

Willow grinned and looked at Rick.

Rick shook his head. "No way. I want the nugget for my
rock collection."

"Don't be mean." Casey gave Rick a push.

Rick staggered and one foot got wet.

"How much longer are you going to be in Dawson?"
Casey continued.

"Dad says a couple more weeks," said Rick.

"So, give the nugget from the raft race to your mom and
we'll go panning on Dad's claim every day until we find one
for your collection."

Visions of riches danced in Rick's head. He'd always
wanted to be a gold miner. "Done," he said.

Willow was looking thoughtful. "When we came up on
the bus, Kate asked us what we wanted to find in the
Klondike. I said adventure — and we've both had that." She

turned to Rick. "You wanted a gold nugget, and now we've both got that."

"Kate wanted big bucks," said Rick. "And she's gone away with even less than she came with."

"So we've both found what we wanted," Willow said. "And Kate's lost her money and her job."

"But she wanted the big bucks just for herself," said Casey. "You've shared what you've found. You gave the ring back to my grandma, and now you're giving your prize nuggets to your mom. And Rick's poem has been shared with everyone in town."

"Yeah," said Rick. "I hope I've heard the last of that one."

"Hey, Rick," called his mom. "Will you do us a favour? Mrs. Eriksen wants to hear 'The Bishop Who Ate His Boots' — again."

AUTHOR'S NOTE

This story is a work of fiction based on a real background. We spent three months in Dawson, Yukon, as writers-in-residence at Berton House. We walked everywhere we could, photographed each other in bright daylight at midnight on the longest day, panned for gold, visited dog mushers and their dogs, and talked to First Nations, historians, kids, miners, and Parks Canada staff.

Dawson in the story is as real as we could make it, and the descriptions of Dredge #4, the Palace Grand Theatre, and Robert Service's cabin are authentic. Service wrote many of his poems as we have described, and Bishop Stringer really ate his boots (though we wrote the poem, in Service style). And the story of the Klondike ring being thrown in the river by a little girl is real, but it was our imagination that had Willow find it — and its original owner — again. Discovery Days is much as we have described it (we rode in the parade), but the raft race was dropped a few years ago and has been revived only in our imaginations. The cabin where Rick found the poem is also a real one — but we don't know that Service was ever there. We didn't look behind the wallboards, so who knows if a poem is really there waiting to be found.

Some of our characters are doing jobs that exist, but all the people are invented and bear no resemblance to people we met in Dawson (or elsewhere). And we have the greatest respect for Parks Canada and are quite sure they wouldn't hire Kate (if she existed).

ABOUT THE AUTHORS

Andrea and David Spalding live on Pender Island, British Columbia. They travel to many parts of Canada doing research for their books and visiting schools. They have three children and seven grandchildren — one of whom lives with them just now, and has enjoyed *The Klondike Ring* as bedtime reading chapter by chapter as it was being written.

Andrea's many books for children include several picture books and novels for readers of various ages. Apart from the Adventure•Net series, she is currently writing *The Summer of Magic* quartet, fantasy novels set in England. She has also written numerous books for adults.

As well as collaborating with Andrea on this series, David has written educational radio for children and also writes books on science for adults, particularly about dinosaurs and whales.

You may contact the Spaldings and find out more about their books through their websites:

www.andreaspalding.com and www.davidspalding.com.

Enjoy all of the books in the Adventure.Net series!

THE LOST SKETCH (#1)
ISBN: 1-55110-989-1

Willow and Rick's expedition at a canoe camp in Ontario takes a turn for the unexpected when they stumble across an abandoned boxcar. Among the cobwebs, they discover a mysterious painting.

THE SILVER BOULDER (#2)
ISBN: 1-55285-105-2

Brother and sister sleuths Rick and Willow are looking for a lost boulder full of silver, as big as a truck. Everyone they meet in Kaslo, British Columbia, seems to have a secret. As they hunt deeper and deeper, they discover disturbing things about the past and try to find a way to help new friends regain what they lost.

THE DISAPPEARING DINOSAUR (#3)
ISBN: 1-55285-311-X

Willow and Rick join a dinosaur dig in Dry Valley, Alberta, where a *Tyrannosaurus rex* skeleton is being excavated. However, the dig seems to be cursed with strange accidents and disappearing equipment. As they dig deeper, Willow and Rick unearth more than just dinosaur bones and discover that some of the workers have something to hide.